Hero and the
Sinking Ships

By the same author and illustrator

Violet and the Mean and Rotten Pirates
Cal and the Amazing Anti-Gravity Machine
Jack Bolt and the Highwaymen's Hideout
Ghostboy and the Moonbalm Treasure

To find out more go to:
www.hamiltonhearnbooks.com

Hero and the Sinking Ships

by Richard Hamilton

illustrated by Sam Hearn

BLOOMSBURY
CHILDREN'S
BOOKS

First published in Great Britain in 2008 by Bloomsbury Publishing Plc
36 Soho Square, London, W1D 3QY

A CIP catalogue record of this book is available from the British Library

ISBN 978 0 7475 9556 4

All papers used by Bloomsbury Publishing are natural, recyclable products
made from wood grown in well-managed forests. The manufacturing processes
conform to the environmental regulations of the country of origin.

Typeset by Dorchester Typesetting Group Ltd
Printed in Great Britain by Clays Ltd, St Ives Plc

1 3 5 7 9 10 8 6 4 2

www.bloomsbury.com

For Alison and Laing – R.H.

For the Cherretts: Ash, Jess, Grace, Olivia and Florence – S.H.

Contents

Chapter One   1
The Morgan Street Rats

Chapter Two   6
The Nest in the Attic

Chapter Three   12
Snowbound

Chapter Four   18
A Slip on the Edge

Chapter Five   25
Slow Snow Journey

Chapter Six   32
To the Port

Chapter Seven   39
Voyaging with Vladimir

Chapter Eight   48
The Little Rats' Plan

Chapter Nine   54
To the Lifeboats!

Chapter Ten   60
At Sea in a Tub

Chapter Eleven   66
A Pocketful of Rats

Chapter Twelve   71
An Idiotic Nest

Chapter Thirteen   77
Beautiful Blossom

Chapter Fourteen   82
The Best Nest

Chapter Fifteen   89
Jim

Chapter Sixteen   95
Reunited

Chapter Seventeen   104
Afternoon Tea

Chapter Eighteen   114
A Dish Served Cold

Chapter Nineteen   119
Saviour and Protector

Chapter Twenty   124
Hero the Human

Chapter Twenty-one   131
The Parents Suffer

Chapter Twenty-two   135
Touché

Chapter Twenty-three   143
Humans v. Animals

Chapter Twenty-four   148
Pig for the Pot

Chapter Twenty-five   153
Trapped

Chapter Twenty-six   159
Cat Fight

Chapter Twenty-seven   166
Then . . .

Chapter Twenty-eight   168
Survivors

Chapter Twenty-nine   176
Surf Rats

Chapter One
The Morgan Street Rats

The Morgan Street Rats had never thought of themselves as unlucky. They lived in the attic of a crumbling Georgian house in a city thronging with gloriously filthy human beings. Downstairs there was a restaurant whose lazy chef left out their supper every night. Roast chicken, apple pie, even fancy French vol-au-vents were theirs for the taking. On top of this there was a dog in the restaurant, who terrified the neighbourhood cats but was far too grand to notice the rats, and let them scamper past his nose with barely a sniff.

So, in the beginning, the rats had a merry old time. They gorged on the food from the restaurant, licked dirty plates at night, ransacked the rubbish, swam in the sink of dirty washing-up water and chewed old fish bones and chicken carcasses to their hearts' content. They liked to stretch out by the dying embers of the restaurant fire, when the diners had left, belching gently after a heavy plum pudding. They loved the fire, its warmth spreading through the bricks of the chimney all the way up the rickety house to their nests in the attic.

The owner of the restaurant, a Mr Tide, didn't care much about the rats. He was a slovenly, long-haired, unshaven man, who drank too much and wore an apron so caked in ancient food that mould grew upon it.

One day a party of lawyers came to lunch and stayed all afternoon celebrating the end of a long trial. They ate mussels and oysters and rabbit pie, followed by an old treacle sponge that the rats had failed to finish off the previous night. A few hours later the lawyers were monstrously sick. Two of them came gasping to the door of the restaurant, desperate with stomach aches and anger. They banged on the door, bellowing and groaning at the owner.

Then they saw the rats, scampering across the

tables, feasting on cheese and pie, gorging on left-over potato salad.

The lawyers' revenge was swift: the following day the restaurant was closed. Mr Tide was thrown in gaol (such is the power of lawyers), the dog was removed to the country, and a new owner arrived. The rats' luck had changed.

The new owner of the restaurant was called Mrs Spark. She wore a starched white apron and she cleaned the premises from top to bottom. She threw out the rotten furniture and scrubbed the floors. She knew there were rats in the attic, so she bought a cat. Not just any old cat – a hunter. A rat-catcher, the best in the business. He was as black as the night, with thin green eyes and claws like sharp-ened fish hooks. His name was Snarl.

In no time Snarl had done his work. On his first night he lay in wait for the rats and pounced. He caught six and lined them up by the back door. The following night he caught another four. The rats knew it was time to move on. They no longer dared go down to the restaurant or sneak out to the rub-bish bins.

Snarl waited for them around every corner, gloat-ing on his success. He hissed into the rat run under the floorboards and smacked his lips. He purred softly, threateningly, into the dark attic at night. His call found its way into the dreams of the rats and unsettled them. So the families of rats departed, frightened and hungry.

All except one. They were a new family and the babies were too young to move. Their eyes were still shut and they lay gulping air and drinking their mother's milk in a little nest under the floorboards of the attic. To keep away from Snarl, they had to move to the very corner of the eaves, to a nook by a wooden beam that was sticking out just under the roof. One side of the nest was actually in the open air next to a terrible three-storey drop to the street below. Pa rat had to use himself as a wall to stop the babies falling out. Wind and rain came in from the outside, while Snarl prowled the inside. It was no place to bring up a family, but Ma rat and Pa rat were stuck with it . . .

Chapter Two
The Nest in the Attic

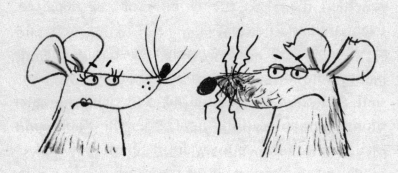

'I'm cold,' complained Ma.

'*You're* cold,' said Pa.

'And I am damp.'

'*You* are damp,' repeated Pa. His eyes were closed. His back was curved next to the drop, holding in the babies and open to the wind and rain. He was colder and damper and more miserable than Ma would ever be. This nest was too small.

'And surely it is about to snow,' said Ma, with a sniff and a little cry.

Pa opened his tiny dark eyes. They glinted in the dull afternoon light, like black beads. His fur twitched around his snout. 'My whiskers are frozen!' he moaned. 'Frozen stiff. Ow! And baby number one is giving me trouble.'

'Baby number four is giving me trouble,' said Ma. 'She has sharp claws.'

'Now number two is facing the wrong way,' said Pa, wriggling. '*I* have no milk,' he told the blind, snuffling little thing.

'But number three is perfect,' said Ma lovingly. 'Good rat! He has positioned himself just right and has sweet milky breath and adorable twitchy paws.'

Pa was quiet. He disapproved of soppiness. Once they were out of the nest, his children would have to deal with the hard knocks of life. The rough and the tumble. Cats and dogs and cockroaches. Not to mention humans. There was no time for soppiness. He nudged baby number two away and with his hind legs pushed number five back from the brink, where she was making a bid for freedom.

'When will these babies' eyes open?' Pa sighed. It was the umpteenth time he had asked the question.

'Soon,' Ma told him. 'It's three weeks tomorrow since they were born. Then they will be ready.'

Pa sighed again. 'If they get any bigger, they'll push me off this ledge. I shall fall to a terrible death in Morgan Street.'

'Don't,' said Ma kindly. 'We need you.'

A flurry of snow billowed in the street below them, blinding the men on the ground and sending a pigeon squawking over the rooftops. A dozen white flakes were suddenly posted like letters into the nest, and lay dissolving on the rats.

'Tssssssssssss,' came a silky hiss from inside the attic.

Ma and Pa looked up. Their fur bristled. It was Snarl. Up to his tricks again. He knew where they were and he enjoyed teasing them.

Scratch, scratch. Snarl was fishing. Scratching at the floorboard, trying to pull it away, trying to get his paw closer to the rats. If he was lucky he might snare one with his claws. He knew they were in there. He could smell them. It was driving him mad with hunger.

'Oh, this is awful,' Ma whimpered. She could hear Snarl's purr now, pulsing through the floorboards. Ma and Pa rat trembled. The bitter east wind whistled under the tiles. It cut through their fur and bone. They trembled with fear and they trembled with cold.

'I can't bear this country any more,' Ma wailed. 'I want to move. I want a new home. A home that is

warm, in a place that is safe.'

Pa blinked away a snowflake. He felt suddenly sad: he was failing his family. He should build a nest in a nice, cosy place. Not here on the edge of a cliff, with a hungry cat smacking his lips outside.

'As soon as the babies can travel,' he told Ma through chattering teeth, 'we shall move.'

'Where to?' asked Ma. 'Tell me.' She longed for Pa to give her hope.

'To somewhere warm. Somewhere where there is proper heat. We shall move . . . to the Tropics,' said Pa decisively. It was the warmest place he could think of.

'Tell me about the Tropics,' Ma asked dreamily.

Pa tried to paint a picture. It would have to be good. It would have to give Ma hope. 'In the Tropics there are warm sleepy lagoons, full of rotting vegetables. There is a delicious steamy heat, heavy with ripe smells. Fruit falls from the trees and rots on the ground. It never, ever snows.'

'Really?' said Ma, brightening.

'Really. Long ago, rats lived in the Tropics. That's where we came from. We came west on ships. West – to this bitter, frozen land. I think we must have come in summer, when it was warm, little knowing the harsh winter that follows.'

'How far away are the Tropics?' asked Ma.

Pa thought. 'A few miles,' he said vaguely. He had a notion that it might be a little further − but he liked to be optimistic.

'Can we really go?' Ma asked.

'Of course! And if rats came from the Tropics in ships − we can go back . . . in ships!' Pa rat shivered off a mantle of snow and rose up suddenly. He would do this. He really would. 'The moment the babies' eyes open,' he declared solemnly, 'I promise that we shall go down to the docks and find a ship to the Tropics!'

Ma opened her eyes and looked lovingly at Pa. 'Yes. Oh yes, please,' she said, with longing. 'And then we can leave the cold and the snow and this beastly cat. Rufus − you are wonderful.'

'Thank you.' Pa smiled, showing his fine buck teeth.

Chapter Three
Snowbound

As soon as the babies' eyes opened, they became interested in the world. They found it a cold, wet frozen place – so they immediately hid from it. They preferred the hairy warmth of their parents' tummies.

Babies numbers one, three and four opened their eyes first, and Ma and Pa duly gave them their names. Number one was called Happy, because she smiled and gurgled in the nest. Baby four was called Scratcher, because her claws were sharp and busy. But they disagreed over baby number three's name.

'He is handsome. So let us call him Rufus.' That was Pa's name (and surprise: it was Pa's suggestion!).

'No, no. I will get terribly confused if you both have the same name,' said Ma. 'This rat has delicate features. He shall be Romeo.'

'Romeo? Too fancy. Too foppish,' Pa declared firmly. He looked into baby number three's eyes. They were lively and daring. They sparkled. 'He has spirit,' agreed Pa. 'He should have a strong name. Something heroic. Like . . . "Hero".'

'Ooooo. Hero. I like that.' Ma gazed at the little rat. 'My Hero,' she giggled.

A day later the other three babies opened their eyes. They were called Solo, Chewy and Morgan. Solo was making a break for freedom even with her eyes shut; Chewy had large early teeth; and Morgan, last to open his eyes, was named after the street.

Once the little rats could see him, Pa decided that he had to make the babies understand that he was their father and he was In Charge. The nest was bright with reflected light from the snow. They lay all together in the deep snow silence; it was a special moment: that of a family looking at each other for the first time.

'Children,' said Pa rat. 'Welcome to the world. Here is my thought for today: we share the world

with many animals, but particularly with our tall, smooth-skinned relatives – the humans. Humans think they rule the world, but they are mistaken. *Always remember: there are more rats than humans.* Now, we love human filth. We love their leftovers, and their rubbish and their houses and their ships. But we don't like *them*. They are bigger than us and they are mean to us – so be careful. They are jealous because *we* are the more successful species!' He laughed.

Blinking their tiny eyes, the rat babies gazed at their father in admiration. They were proud to be rats.

'*My* thought for the day,' said Ma, once the babies had digested Pa's stirring words, 'is, *Beware* of the perilous drop on the other side of your father – it's three floors down to the street and you won't survive. *Beware* of cats. In the room behind me there is a hungry cat called Snarl who likes nothing better than a baby rat for tea. *Beware* of eating anything too solid – like wood or bone or glass – it will give you a horrid tummy ache. And finally – don't worry about the cold, because your father and I have decided that soon we are moving to the Tropics, where the rubbish floats in tepid lagoons and the air is moist and full of decay.'

'Hee hee, hee hee,' laughed the babies, all snuggling together.

The following night was bitterly cold and though the babies were safe and warm, by the morning Pa was half-dead with icicles hanging off his back. Snow was falling heavily, choking up the streets and alleys half as high as a horse. The baby rats hunkered down in the nest, drinking milk and growing stronger.

Three days later, in the evening, such a hunger seized Pa that he ventured out in search of food. The cat Snarl had been quiet for some time and Pa decided he must risk it, for the sake of Ma and the babies.

He left Ma lying in his place by the drop, keeping the children in the nest. He felt his way along the rat run under the floorboards with his whiskers and his nose. He sniffed. Cold north wind, the smell of snow. He listened. Silence. He peeped out – unfortunately he couldn't see much as he had terrible eyesight. There was a great deal of dark and gloom.

'Yioaw!!' snarled a cat suddenly and as Pa ducked

down, a paw caught him on the spine. Snarl! He had been hiding downwind, silent and still as a statue. Snarl had known that sooner or later the rats would have to come out. He flexed his paws and his sharp claws splayed into the rat's fur.

Pa quickly twisted round and bit the paw. He tasted the sweet blood as Snarl yelped and let go. Pa squirmed away, down under the floorboards, his heart pounding with shock and fear. The cat's head and sharp teeth came after him, hissing . . . but got caught in the hole, and yowled in frustration.

'Go and find a measly mouse for tea,' Pa growled, backing away from the cat's head. He scurried back thankfully to the safety of the nest, his tummy still rumbling with hunger.

Chapter Four
A Slip on the Edge

'Snarl is on the prowl,' he told Ma, when he returned to the nest and took his place by the eaves. They shuffled around each other. 'How are we *ever* going to get out of here?' Pa groaned. He stuck his back half out of the edge of the nest and relaxed.

But in his absence a slippery patch of ice had formed by the drop and Pa felt himself begin to slide. 'Woah!' he exclaimed in surprise. He was trying to wriggle back, when suddenly his hind legs slipped right out over the drop.

'Help!' He scrabbled desperately. 'I'm going – WHAA . . .!' Suddenly his whole body slipped out of the nest and he was left hanging on with his front claws digging into the roof timber. His face popped up. 'Help me, I'm slipping!' he squeaked.

'Rufus!' cried Ma, seeing her mate disappearing out into the snowy world.

'I'm off!' he said, his eyes wider than she had ever seen. Beneath him his feet scrabbled in mid-air. Ma caught his paw.

'Pa!' cried Hero and Scratcher.

'Oh, darlings – your very first words!' squealed Ma and, delighted at their swift progress, she let go of Pa and turned to her babies.

'That's it,' cried Pa. 'I'm flying – Good-byeeeeeeeee . . .' His voice faded away.

And he was gone. Lost in the snowbound street far below.

Ma stared into the darkness that had swallowed up Pa. Her lip quivered. 'Are you there?' she called into the darkness. There was no reply, just the bitter, whistling wind.

'Poor Pa,' she whispered sadly. She found herself fighting back tears. She saw how the ice was slippery at the edge and she blamed herself for not seeing it. Now her children were fatherless. And it

was her fault. 'I wonder if we'll see him ever again?' She felt so alone. Family life had been so sweet. And so short.

'Aahhh!' Hero shrieked – a tiny baby shriek – and suddenly he was gone too! Ma glimpsed her baby rat flying through the air to the ground below.

'Oh, disaster! Oh, careless children – beware! I said, beware!' Ma herded her remaining offspring back from the edge. 'Beware the edge! Does no one listen? A father and a baby in one minute, lost.' Her beautiful baby too. Ma felt the pain of loss and her eyes welled up with tears. Careless mother! What a stupid place to build a nest! What did she think she was – a bird?

As Pa fell he was convinced it was the end of him. He spiralled through the air, glimpsing the gables of the houses and St Paul's Church and the bright light of the silvery moon. *Goodbye*, he thought and then he said his last words, which were, perhaps surprisingly, 'No more pudding.'

But instead of smashing into the hard pavement, he was plunged into a comfortable pillow of snow. Snow filled his eyes and his mouth and his nostrils and slid past his tummy and in between his claws as he travelled down, deep down, into the middle of a drift. When he stopped, he lay thinking: *I am alive.* And then he thought with glee: *Roly-poly pudding for me!*

'Ha ha!' he laughed, spitting out the crystals of snow. He peered up. He could see the tunnel he had come through, all the way up to the sky. And by it must be the house.

'Helloooooo!' he called.

And, as if in answer, a small furry thing flew down the tunnel and hit him on the nose.

'Hello, Pa!' said the thing.

'Hero!' cried Pa, dusting off his nose. 'What are you doing here?'

'I slipped and fell.' At a very early age Hero realised that not all things your parents tell you are true: contrary to his mother's warning, he had survived the fall.

'Oh. I see.' Pa shrugged. 'I slipped and fell too. The thing is, Hero,' Pa grew serious, 'we are rats not bats. We were not meant to fly. I should have told you that.'

'But, Pa – I had the softest landing. I want to do it again, it was so fun.'

'Such fun,' corrected Pa. And then he had an idea.

'DAAARRLING!'

Far above Ma replied. He could hear the surprise in her voice.

'We're alive!' he shouted.

A moment later there was a squeak from high above and Scratcher came tumbling into the snowdrift, swiftly followed by Morgan.

'Hello, children,' said Pa, wiping the snow from his eyes again. 'Your mother is a genius and a mind-reader. I was going to suggest she send you down.'

'Rufus – the babies – I'm losing the babies!' shouted Ma, panicking up above.

'It's all right. I have them. I –'

There was a long descending chorus of squeaks and suddenly four more rats came plummeting one after the other into the snow.

'Hello, everybody,' said Pa, when they had all arrived. He smiled broadly. 'Quite a party.'

'Is this what they mean by a snow-hole?' asked Ma, when she had recovered.

'Indeed – it is a sort of igloo,' said Pa, pleased that things had worked out so well.

'It dark,' said Chewy.

'It *is* dark,' corrected Pa.

'I said that,' said Chewy, lifting his lip into a sneer.

Pa sniffed. He could see Chewy was going to be difficult.

'I suggest,' he told them all, 'that we see if we can find an entrance to the drains. Humans always flush their waste out to the river, so if we follow the drains we must eventually come to the river. The river leads to the sea and the sea leads . . . to the Tropics.'

'Our journey to a warm place has begun!' Ma cried with pleasure.

They each took hold of the tail in front of them and with Pa leading the way and Ma behind, they began to tunnel through the snow in the direction of what they *thought* was the drain.

Chapter Five
Slow Snow Journey

The snow tunnel seemed to go on a long way. Pa joked that after behaving like bats, and flying through the air, they were now behaving like moles, and tunnelling. He told the babies that this wasn't normal rat behaviour, but at least it was Crafty. And Craftiness was very typical rat behaviour. And to be encouraged.

And then Pa bumped into something with his nose. 'It's a wall,' he told them. The way to the Tropics was blocked.

Unfortunately the snow also blocked all sound from travelling the length of six baby rats in a snow tunnel. So they whispered their father's message along the row. (And as you know from the game 'Chinese whispers', messages can easily become garbled when whispered along a row.)

'It's a wall' became 'He's had a fall'.

From the back Ma replied, 'Is he hurt?' Which became 'Stay alert', which became 'Mind the dirt', which arrived at Pa as: 'What's for dessert?'

Pa was confused. 'There's no food here. We have to go back.'

Which was passed down the line. 'Go back' became 'have a crack', and so on until Ma received the final communication: 'We've got to attack!'

Alarmed, Ma rose up and shouted lustily, 'Attack? I'm behind you! Attack! Attack!' She had a strong desire to protect her offspring (fuelled by the guilt that she felt after allowing them to fall from the attic) and she rushed forward and caught up with Pa.

'Whom are we attacking?' she cried, baring her formidable teeth. 'Is that cat there?'

'No one,' said Pa, turning round and round in confusion. 'I said, we've got to go *back*.'

At this point they heard a rough, deep voice that came from somewhere near the wall and made them stop, and stand as still as stones.

'What's all the rumpus?' growled the voice.

It was a big brown rat, the kind that lived in drains and cellars.

'We are looking for the way to the quay,' Pa told the rat. 'We've a ship to catch.'

'Follow the wall,' replied the brown rat gruffly, 'there's a drain at the end. It flows to the ditch, which flows to the river. Which flows, as you know, to the sea.'

'Thanks a million,' said Pa.

Pa and his family tunnelled their way through the snow to the drain. At last they found the pipe and once inside they were free from the cold snow. Here it was dark and smelly and they loved it. Only Hero complained.

'It stinky,' he said.

'It *is* stinky. And what a rich stink it is. A drain like this is worth lingering in,' Pa told him. 'The stinkier the better. In the hot weather a drain like this would make your whiskers curl!'

They scurried through the darkness, claws slipping on the muddy gunge, through puddles of rotten vegetable juices and tangles of hair matted with slime.

'Not a lot of food in here,' Pa explained, sniffing a mouldy eggshell, 'but always worth investigating a drain. If you're lucky you might find an old bone, or a crust of bread or something.'

The little rats sniffed the grunge. Solo found a chicken leg. Chewy found a bit of old basket.

'No, darling,' said Ma. 'That's not very nice to eat.'

'It is,' said Chewy, with his mouth full.

'Hey! That's mine!' cried Solo, as Hero chewed the other end of the chicken bone.

'No! This end is mine!' cried Hero. 'You got that end.'

'Solo *was* there first,' said Ma reasonably.

'But a chicken bone has two ends!' squeaked Hero.

'Share. Share,' said Pa, hovering nearby. 'We must share among the family.'

'Then I want the middle,' said Scratcher, rushing in and locking her little teeth round the middle of the bone.

'Hey!' the other two objected.

'Ah – no – what I meant . . .' began Pa.

'Chicken bone! Chicken bone!' cried all the other little rats and surged around the bone, trying to get a piece of the action.

Ma looked hard at Pa. 'We have to agree to say the same thing,' she snapped.

Pa nodded. 'Solo *was* there first,' he said, too late. This parenting lark was trickier than he had thought.

As they journeyed on, their pipe grew into a bigger pipe. A short way after that, it led to a ditch and the ditch to a stream and more snow.

It was almost light now, and the rats had to be careful. They ran in a little line along the muddy, snow-slushy bank of the river, keeping all the time to the side of rocks or pieces of wood, half seeing, half smelling their way. Hero breathed in the fresh air and felt good.

'Pretend to be shadows,' Ma told them, 'here one moment, gone the next. Quicker than the blink of an eye.'

The little rats tried: they all ran off in different directions, jumping and laughing for joy.

'STOP!' cried Pa, rearing up on his hind legs. 'Come back! You've got to stay together,' he told them firmly. 'It is the number one family rule! Otherwise you'll get lost and . . .' He paused. There was no way to explain gently: 'Eaten.'

'*Eaten?*' squeaked Hero.

'That's right. It is a tough world out there.'

The rats looked at each other, their little black eyes wide at the thought.

'What's being eaten feel like?' asked Morgan slowly.

Pa worried about Morgan. 'Nobody has ever been able to say,' he told him darkly.

The family pressed on. They passed under the hulls of boats drawn up on the muddy shore. Some smelled temptingly of old fish and barnacles, others of sand and rock. Some of the boats were passenger boats, with the humans' sweet stink. The rats saw crabs and shells and rocks as they slipped and slid along the icy shoreline. They wanted to stay and explore the world, but their parents were constantly urging them on.

Chapter Six
To the Port

Soon they came to the big river, a thick brown serpent stretching further than they could see. They ran up to the wharf, where all the ships' cargo was unloaded. Now all was clean and white with a dusting of snow that picked out the scene like a pencil drawing.

They ran over the slippery timbers, leaving little tracks behind them. They scampered through the stacked packing cases and flapping canvas tarpaulins, past coils of thick rope, into the forest of creaking ships' masts lined up along the quay.

Ma found a dry spot near some sacking. It was out of the raw wind and they squeezed in together for warmth. Pa went off to see if he could find some food.

'I'm so cold,' said Scratcher, shivering, 'let me in.' The little rats parted a bit to give her space.

'We need thicker fur,' said Hero, feeling the cold on his exposed back.

'Look.' Chewy was gnawing into the sacking. He had a mouth full of thick hemp threads. 'Food,' he told them.

The others found the sacking tasteless. But behind the sacking they found cotton, tightly packed into a bale. They began pulling out white tufts.

'It's like snow,' said Happy.

'Only warm,' cried Solo.

'I will cover myself in it,' said Hero, burrowing into it. 'No one can see me,' he laughed, peeping out of a cotton wig and beard. He liked the warmth too.

Pa returned looking rather pleased. 'You'll never believe it,' he began, pausing to regard Hero. He had never seen a rat cover himself in cotton. 'I have just met a cousin of mine.'

Ma laughed. Pa was always running into cousins.

'His name is Vladimir. He says we can have a

berth on his boat while we search for a ship to the Tropics.'

'Can we bring our cotton?' Hero asked.

Pa didn't think this was proper rat behaviour. 'There is already a nest,' he explained. 'Come on, quick, let's go before someone else gets there before us.'

So Hero reluctantly left his cotton and followed his family along the quay to the ship of Pa's cousin, Vladimir. A seagull watched them pass. Ma watched the gull, her teeth and claws at the ready. The gull pretended not to be interested in a troupe of little rats and hopped off. But Ma kept watching. You never knew with seagulls.

The ship that Vladimir lived in was an antique three-masted sloop with any number of entrances for crafty rats. Pa headed straight for the thick rope securing the ship to the quay and they teetered along it, hopped on to the deck and down a hole into the hold. Pa slipped along a slanting crossbeam. 'Watch out for splinters,' he warned, and in a second they were deposited – to their surprise – in an incredibly warm nest.

'Wowee!' the little rats cried.

It was like being plunged into a sweet-smelling hayloft in the middle of summer, straight from bleak midwinter. The warmth, the cosiness, the luxury made the little rats squeal with delight and curl their tiny paws. Ma beamed: Pa had certainly come up trumps this time. It was a splendid nest.

'Vladimir!' Pa called his cousin. There was a shuffling noise behind a panel and a large elderly rat popped his head out. He squinted at them with his old watery eyes.

'Roger,' he began.

'Rufus,' Pa corrected him.

'Rufus,' Vladimir began again. 'Don't –' He sighed suddenly as if the effort of what he was about to say was too much. 'Oh – make yourself at home,' he told them. It was easier than telling them what *not* to do. He disappeared and then reappeared (Happy found this funny and squeaked with laughter).

'Roger,' began Vladimir (the little rats sniggered).

'Rufus,' Pa corrected him again.

'Rufus – remind me again, you are Mary's . . . sister's father's cousin's son's daughter's third son.'

'That is the sum of it!' agreed Pa nimbly, with a wink to Ma.

Ma rolled her eyes.

'Good good,' mumbled Vladimir, waving his whiskers. They seemed to act independently of the rest of him, like tentacles of seaweed waving in the current. 'Er . . . welcome.' He disappeared.

'Where *does* he go to?' whispered Ma.

'The galley pipe,' Pa replied. 'It is always hot and the old boy likes to warm his backside on it.' Pa looked around at their new nest. He smirked at everyone. 'Hey – this is all right! Isn't it?'

'This is fantastic!' squealed Happy, stretching her paws in the air.

'It's brilliant,' sang Hero. He put his snout in the air and sniffed. He could smell old rats and sweet humans and fish and tar and ropes.

'Is this going to the Tropics?' asked Solo.

'No, no,' explained Pa. 'This ship is moored. We are only taking shelter here while we find a ship that *is* going to the Tropics.'

'Are there any other rats here?' asked Scratcher.

Pa laughed. 'In this old tub? Certainly not. Rats are always the first to leave a sinking ship. We know a ship is going to go down long before the foolish humans. We know when a ship is seaworthy and when it is not. And this ship is NOT seaworthy. Oh no. This ship is rotten. Only a mad rat – or a mad human – would put to sea in *this* leaky tub!'

'Is Vladimir mad?' asked Hero

'Well, yes,' said Ma kindly. 'A little.'

Pa then told the little rats how to tell whether a ship was seaworthy. They had to listen to the creaks and the groans of the ship's timbers and the sloshing of too much water in the bilges. They had to feel how damp the wood was, and to look out for telltale stains and leaks. But he reassured them that so long as this ship was moored up, it was perfectly safe and made a fine shelter from foul weather.

Which was why, when they heard a loud splash and the ship lurched suddenly to the side, tipping the little rats out of the warm nest, Ma and Pa jumped up in alarm.

The ship had set sail!

Chapter Seven
Voyaging with Vladimir

'Where are we going? Where are we going?' cried the little rats excitedly.

'I don't know,' said Pa, clutching his stomach, which was doing odd topsy-turvy things. 'Not far I trust.'

Up on deck came a series of shouts: 'Haul the anchor! Take her up, Mister Bo'sun!'

'Weeeeeeee!' Chewy and Hero tumbled out of the bedding.

'I feel sick,' groaned Morgan.

Ma nuzzled him gently. 'Surely it is just a change of position,' she said. 'They must be moving the ship along the quay a little bit.'

A bell sounded above them, and they heard an odd animal grunting.

Vladimir put his head around the corner. 'Along the quay did you say, Roger? Not at all. Ha ha! We've set sail! We are going on a voyage to MUR-MANSK!' he boomed. 'A month and a half at sea!'

'Murmansk?' cried Pa. 'But we want to go to the Tropics.'

'Is it cold in Murmansk?' asked Hero, looking at his parents.

'Cold?' hooted Vladimir. 'It is *perishing* in Murmansk. It will freeze your little tails off! It is in *Russia*! The port is practically an iceberg!' His whiskers waved like insect antennae.

'Oh,' wailed Ma, hiding her head in her front paws. 'I can't bear it. I want to go somewhere warm! I'm not a penguin! I can't make a home on an iceberg.'

'But this ship isn't in a state to go to sea.' Pa clutched his churning stomach. 'Listen to the creaks and groans. We might as well go to sea in a . . . a . . .'

'In a bucket,' honked Vladimir. He collapsed in laughter. 'In half a bucket! But at least we have it to ourselves, eh?'

Pa's mouth opened and closed. It was no use

arguing with Vladimir. He had one idea of life, and Pa had another. Pa looked to the future. He looked at his family. *I must not show my fear, because that would frighten the little ones. I must not be seasick either,* he thought queasily.

'Maybe . . . we shall be . . . blown off course . . . into the Tropics?' he suggested hopefully.

Ma looked at him. She liked his optimism, but on important points she believed in telling the truth. 'If the ship sinks, children, head for the lifeboats,' she told them.

What a splendid adventure, thought the little rats.

Over the next two days the ship sailed north, and Pa and Ma got to know their offspring a little better. They gave them permission to explore the ship, provided they kept returning to check in with their parents.

Chewy and Happy and Scratcher went off together, in a little pack. They scampered through the hull looking for food. They enjoyed chewing through rotten wooden panels into new parts of the ship that might hold something to eat.

Morgan liked to stay with Ma and Pa. He followed them wherever they went. He was a dependent rat and Ma liked that and took special care of him.

Hero and Solo were different. They were independent rats, and went off exploring on their own. Solo disappeared to the dark places near the bilges. She found that she liked to sit and think in the darkness. She liked to listen to the splash and suck of the waves against the hull.

Hero also liked to sit and think, but he was drawn to the open air, to the light. He was an adventurous rat and soon began to find his way along the old abandoned rat runs around the ship.

On the first day he looked out at the cold grey sea and the disappearing land. He found a hole leading into a cupboard in the galley, filled with pots and pans, and another into the sailors' mess room. He popped his head out of a hole on deck and saw the sails stretching like clouds above him. He was so curious that he decided there and then that he wanted to see everything in the whole world. And then he saw the humans.

Hero was amazed by the humans. By their size, their strength. Their *presence*. The master of the ship was a big, burly man called Oleg Olegovitch. He

had long black hair and a thick black beard and he would sail a soup tureen through a hurricane if there were money in it.

Hero watched Oleg shouting orders into the cold wind, his hand on the wheel, his feet planted squarely on the deck. There was something magnificent about him – about his sheer size. He was fifty – no, a hundred – times the size of the little rat. He may have been rough and salty, but Hero also saw something tender in the sea captain's eyes, and was drawn to it.

Oleg Olegovitch had filled the ship with wool and candles and oil lamps – things much needed in the northern city of Murmansk. But his most-prized cargo was a beautiful pig called Blossom.

From a little hole by the mast, Hero watched the sea captain and Blossom. Housed on deck, in an upturned, propped-up lifeboat lined with wool (more of a bedroom than a pigsty), Blossom was big and pink and hairy and had a brown mole on her snout. Her teeth were yellow and her breath was sour, but Oleg treated her like a princess.

Hero watched Oleg feed Blossom dainty bits of biscuit and beef, which he had saved from his own plate. 'Oh, my beautiful Blossom,' crooned Oleg, as the pig gobbled up the food in her huge dribbling, toothy mouth.

Hero imagined what it was like to be the favourite of the captain – to be sung to and fed morsels. He thought it looked wonderful, and that night, curled up in the warm nest, he even dreamed he was a pig . . .

While the babies were happily scampering about, Ma and Pa were consumed by worry. Not only was the ship unseaworthy, but they were headed in the wrong direction.

'When the ship puts into port, we must disembark immediately. Then maybe we will find a ship that is heading south,' Pa said.

'We are not stopping,' Vladimir told them from behind the galley pipe. 'We are in a hurry. The ship has to reach Murmansk before the sea freezes over.'

'The sea freezes over?' Ma wailed, horror-struck. She knew it was cold but the thought of the sea freezing over was . . . unthinkable. She gazed at Pa, unable to believe this was true.

'That's right. And it's dark six months of the year! We shall be staying in Murmansk until the spring,' the old rat Vladimir cackled.

'There must be *something* we can do.' Pa scratched his ears nervously. 'There must be *some* way of stopping this ship.' His tail waved from side to side. 'Maybe we shall need to put into port, perhaps to do some repairs?'

Ma looked downcast.

'Repairs?' laughed Vladimir. 'This captain won't put into port for repairs until the water is gushing in!'

Ma closed her eyes and sighed. She felt that she was filling up with sadness.

Pa shuffled off down the passage to find a place to think. 'If at first you don't succeed, try, try again,' he muttered. The trip to the Tropics was going horribly wrong. They were doing the opposite to what he had planned. A frozen wasteland like Murmansk would kill them. They had to do something.

The little rats looked at each other. They could see Ma and Pa were deeply unhappy, and a gloom descended on them.

'. . . *There must be some way of stopping this ship . . .*'

Pa's words echoed through their minds. They huddled together in the nest, their tails and their whiskers twitching and coiling.

'We must help Ma and Pa,' said Morgan.

'I don't want to go to Murmansk,' complained Scratcher.

'If we could only make the captain put into port to repair the ship,' said Solo thoughtfully. She had been listening carefully to Vladimir. 'Then we could catch a different ship . . .'

'It has to be a big repair,' said Happy.

'Like a hole,' Chewy mumbled.

'A hole,' repeated Hero. His eyes lit up as he looked round at his brothers and sisters.

'So the water comes in!' they all cried in a chorus of squeaks. 'Enough to put us into port!'

The little rats squealed with excitement at the prospect of being able to help their loving parents, and off they scampered through the hull, delighted with their plan.

Chapter Eight
The Little Rats' Plan

The little rats ran this way and that, jostling along the old rat runs, squeezing through the old rat holes, tumbling one after the other across the slippery beams, down, down, down into the smelly bottom of the ship.

The timbers were rotten down here. They could feel them under their paws: they were spongy and slimy with seaweed that grew in the dark. They found water oozing through the wooden hull and collecting in the bilges, where it slopped and slapped against the sides of the ship.

'This is a good place,' said Hero, sniffing with his snout a patch of darker wood. It was near an opening above them, and just visible in the gloom. Chewy sniffed the wood too, prodded it with a claw, then began to nibble. The others gathered around and watched. Chewy spat out splinters of wood.

'It's quite soft,' he said, his face twitching with pleasure. 'I think I can bite a little hole here.'

'It'll take more than one of us,' Hero said. 'We all have to do it. Lots of nibbles will make a good-sized hole.'

The little rats lined up in a row all along a plank, and began to nibble the wooden hull. Their teeth bit into the wood, leaving nibble marks all along.

'Hey!' cried Happy, chomping the wood. 'It's salty-tasting.'

'Ummm. Mine is salty too,' declared Scratcher. 'And wet.'

'Look, I got a drip,' cried Morgan excitedly, jumping up and down.

'Me too!' cried Hero. 'I've got two drips!'

'I got a drip too!' chimed in Happy, laughing.

'*I* got a drip-drip-drip!' boasted Solo.

Everyone stopped and looked at Solo's drip-drip-drip. It was impressive. But not enough to stop a ship. The little rats returned to their separate nibblings. Each wanted to be the first to make a significant hole. It didn't take long.

'Ah-ha!' shouted Scratcher excitedly. 'I got a drip-drip-drip *and* a trickle-trickle!'

'You got a trickle — I've got a pour-pouring,' squeaked Happy, waggling her rear in a triumphant dance.

'I've got a spurt!'

'Wee-hee! Me too! Spurt-spurt!'

Suddenly all the rats had a spurting and they stood back to admire their handiwork. They laughed to see one end of the plank spraying impressively while at the other a fountain fired into the air and splashed into the water of the bilges with a satisfying splooshing noise.

'Ha ha!' Happy lay on her back and kicked her legs in pleasure.

CRACK!

Suddenly the little rats fell silent. The crack seemed ominous. It suggested to them that something rather bigger than they had intended was about to happen. And they were right.

CA-BOOOOSH!

Water burst into the bilges — buckets of it, bathfuls of it, *pondfuls* of freezing salty ocean. It roared

and churned through the bottom of the ship, and soon the little rats were looking upon a large foaming pool of water that was rising steadily.

'Oo-er,' said Chewy nervously.

'That's a leak,' said Scratcher.

'Mummy!' squeaked Morgan.

Above them, they heard shouts from the sailors. The ship began to heel over, accompanied by a long, loud creaking, as the water sloshed alarmingly around the bottom and surged towards them.

'Quick, go back!' shouted Hero. He leaped up a beam to a rat hole above. He scrambled through and shot along the run to another hole on another deck. *Help, help,* he cried out to himself. The others followed, running, ears flat, eyes wide with alarm, senses bristling.

They could hear Ma and Pa calling and they called back as they ran, screeching as loudly as they could. All around them there was pandemonium: sailors running here and there, Captain Oleg barking orders, Blossom the pig squealing. By the galley pipe Vladimir was braying, 'We're doomed! We're doomed! Doomed to a watery grave!'

No more pudding, thought Pa.

'Quick, kids.' Ma swiftly counted her babies. The

ship listed in the water. They were going down. She narrowed her eyes. 'Where have you been?' she asked.

The little rats tried not to meet her gaze. They looked at their feet. They studied the knots in the wood around them. Pa's head rose up and studied his children. He bristled.

'Did we stop the ship?' asked Morgan.

'Will we put into port?' asked Chewy.

Pa's eyes suddenly popped. 'Idiots!' he shouted and began hopping from foot to foot. '*You* did this?'

'They're not idiots! *You're* the idiot!' Ma wheeled on him. '*You* were the one who wanted to stop the ship. You gave them the idea!'

'But I didn't gnaw a hole in the hull! *They* did! Idiots!' he bellowed again, hopping up and down with anger, clenching and unclenching his claws.

The little rats quivered with fear.

'Stop it!' pleaded Ma. 'The ship is sinking – never mind who did it – we've got to find the lifeboats. Follow me.'

Chapter Nine
To the Lifeboats!

'Lifeboats!' cried Captain Oleg Olegovitch.

'Are there any?' asked the first mate.

Oleg paused. 'I am thinking . . . One,' he said. 'Lifeboat!' he cried lustily.

The crew ran to Blossom's sty, the upturned, propped-up dingy. Slipping and sliding as the ship pitched in the waves, they struggled with one end and then the other, trying to pick it up and turn it over.

Blossom honked with unhappiness. They were taking her house. Her house was her home. It had snug wool walls. Where was she to go *now*?

As the sailors turned her house over and it slid

across the deck, water broke over the stern and the sails above flapped and snapped and whipped back and forth in the wind. It was a mariner's nightmare – they were sinking.

Ma and Pa and the little rats gathered on deck, hiding in a corner, unseen. Hearts thumping. Legs trembling. Blossom's sty, the wool-lined lifeboat, was before them.

'That's the lifeboat,' said Pa.

'*That?*' squealed Ma. She saw that it must be: the sailors were getting ready to launch it. 'Come on, kids. When I run – you follow.'

They would have to time their run exactly. The side of the ship was listing into the sea as they took on water. When the sailors prepared to lift the boat, Ma shot across the deck and the little rats followed, Pa behind them.

They ran beneath the boat, under the noses of the panicky sailors, to the other side, by the sea. Ma paused. She made sure they had all arrived. A wave suddenly broke over them and sluiced over the deck, almost washing them away. Shaking the water off, the rats scrambled up under a canvas tarpaulin, falling into Blossom's nest of wool, in the boat.

'One–two–three–four–five–six' counted Ma.

'Weeeeheee,' laughed the little rats, tumbling through the wool.

'Be quiet!' Pa ordered. 'This is not funny!' He herded them all to the back of the boat, to a place under a sail, between some shoes and a tool bag. They burrowed down into the sheep's wool. *What a time to have babies*, he thought. *Why didn't we have them at the end of the journey, not at the beginning?*

'We're safe here,' he told them, but he knew they weren't.

The little rats looked up at their pa. They tried hard to make their faces sorrowful. They looked at the deck and their whiskers drooped. 'We're sorry . . . Sorry, Pa . . . Sorry,' they said in dribs and drabs.

Pa's heart melted. But he wouldn't show it. 'Idiots,' he sniffed.

'Abandon ship!' cried Oleg Olegovitch. The crew lifted the lifeboat and slid it awkwardly over the side of the ship. It landed with a splash in the sea and the rats cried out in fear.

Hero's face was jammed into Chewy's armpit. Solo was nose to nose with Morgan. Scratcher's face was by Happy's hind feet. Solo sat on Hero's whiskers.

'Where's Vladimir?' asked Scratcher.

'Try not to think about it,' whispered Ma.

'He's doomed,' said Solo, rolling her eyes.

'We don't know that,' said Pa. 'Maybe he'll pop up somewhere. Now, everyone be quiet and let us hope that no one finds us. Pretend you are . . . shoes. And stay absolutely still.'

Each of the little rats imagined being a shoe, with laces or buckles or smart leather soles. They imagined lying still under a bed or in a suitcase or in the bottom of a boat.

The lifeboat dipped and rose and swayed on the waves.

Happy giggled. 'I got a smelly foot in me,' she said, and Chewy sniggered.

Ma and Pa snuggled up close. They felt so vulnerable. It wouldn't take much for a sailor to lift up the canvas, fiddle around with the tool bag and find them hiding there . . .

Sponge pudding, thought Pa, *and custard. Oh.* Above them, he heard Captain Oleg.

'Wait! Please – no moving! I will not be leaving my beautiful Blossom!'

Pa wondered what the captain was shouting about.

'Bl . . . ooomin' Blossom!' swore a sailor under his breath.

Suddenly a squealing porker came flying through the air and landed with an awful thump in the boat. Her fall was broken by the middle seat, and the middle seat was broken by her fall. The rats screamed, Blossom squealed, the sailors cursed, Pa spun round and round and covered his ears, and Oleg climbed down and took his place.

'Brave Blossom,' he cooed into the pig's ear.

'We shall sink with this fat pig on board,' com-plained a sailor, pushing off from the ship with his oar.

'My pig — she is going with me,' growled Oleg, his eyes blazing. He dared them to challenge him.

The sailors rowed away from the ship, pausing only to watch as the rotten hulk disappeared beneath the waves, taking the candles and wool and oil lamps to the bottom of the sea. They were alone. Five sailors, eight rats and a pig. In a lifeboat.

Chapter Ten
At Sea in a Tub

The little rats shrank into the smallest things they could be, pressed against the side of the boat, hidden under the wool and the canvas sail. The lifeboat rose and sank in the swell. The sailors argued about the direction they should row in. The pig sniffed and snuffled. From their hiding place, the little rats watched a long pink thing flickering and steaming behind Pa's head.

A long pink thing? Steaming? As they were watching it and wondering what it might be, it suddenly lengthened towards them, like a snake.

'Eek,' cried Scratcher, her eyes wide in alarm.

Beyond the long pink thing, they saw the unmistakable sight of Blossom's wet snout, truffling under the sail.

'Eeek – a tongue. A pig's tongue!' squealed Scratcher.

'Piggy wig!' squeaked Chewy, baring his teeth.

'Oh, disgusting!' hollered Ma.

Blossom's vast hairy snout snuffled into their hiding place. Her tongue flickered out, lick-licking. The little rats bared their claws – but Ma was already there: her head shot forward and she bit the wet, snuffling snout. Hard.

Blossom erupted into a deafening, high-pitched screech of pain. She backed away from the rats straight into Captain Oleg, pushing him overboard and then wheeling around among the sailors, who were trying to row the boat.

'Man overboard!' cried a sailor.

'The pig!' yelled another. 'Look out!'

In their hiding place the rats heard a splintering of wood. There were cries as the men stopped rowing, and someone bellowed crazily, 'Stupid swine! It has put its stupid trotter through the hull!'

'Help me!' cried Oleg, floundering in the water.

'The pig was after my babies,' explained Ma.

'Ai-ai-ai-ai-ai!' moaned Pa. 'We're going to sink.'

'Again,' added Hero.

'Pa, is there a lifeboat for the lifeboat?' asked Morgan.

'No such luck,' Pa told him. The image of a treacle pudding sprang into his mind.

Hero peeped out from under the canvas. He could see the pig squealing, its right front trotter had passed straight through a weak section of the boat. Water was gushing in around the trotter. As Hero watched, Captain Oleg burst from the sea like a wild merman.

'A ship,' he spluttered, pointing, 'I am seeing a ship in the east. Row to it, my good lads – we are being saved. Lady Luck is with us.'

The sailors looked out at the horizon and cried out and held their heads. 'The pig has put her hoof through the hull,' they told the captain despairingly. 'She is stuck and we are sinking!'

'But the ship –' Oleg bobbed up and down in the water. 'We still row to it.' He gestured behind him. 'Fifteen minutes only. Please, my good lads – we must be trying – or dying, trying. Eh?'

'Row,' prayed Pa, 'row, you lazy lumps –'

Oleg struggled on board dripping with sea-water. He took charge of Blossom, pulled out her hoof and pushed a rolled-up coat into the hole. But the water still slowly seeped in.

The sailors rowed desperately. They bailed water furiously. The rats kept still. Cold sea-water slopped over their paws and licked their bellies and the little ones moaned. Spying a sailor's pocket nearby, Hero asked Ma if he could hide there.

Ma nodded, pleased with his craftiness. 'Go on,' she whispered, 'Good luck.' How soon her babies were showing signs of independence, she thought.

So Hero, and then Solo and Chewy climbed up and wriggled into the sailor's pocket. They curled up in the dark, dry interior of the sweet-smelling, tobacco-reeking pocket, and waited.

Now Pa and Ma and the others wondered where they could go. Water was slopping around them. If the boat sank, the sea was so very big and they were so very small. They couldn't swim far.

'What should we do, Pa?' asked Morgan.

'My thought for the day is this,' said Pa slowly, giving himself time to think. 'In life, when you see an opportunity . . . grab it!'

'Better still,' said Ma, 'make *your own* opportunity, and grab it.'

The sailors rowed and bailed. They rowed, and they bailed . . . and soon they were close enough to

halloo the ship. They cupped their hands and shouted all together: 'Heeeeeelllllllllllllllppppppp!!!!'

'Grab a hold of anything you can,' cried Pa to his children, 'but get on board that ship!'

The next moment the ship was upon them, bearing down as big as a cathedral. It was a three-masted clipper ship, 500 tons of crafted oak and canvas, ploughing proudly through the ocean. It had shiny brass portholes, splendid white sails and a magnificent figurehead of a lion with a fish in its mouth. Oleg and the sailors gaped.

'Grab her!' cried Oleg. 'Embrace her!' So as the clipper swept past, the sailors grabbed hold of the rigging and began to clamber aboard.

In the confusion, no one saw Pa, brazen as can be, sitting on the shoulder of another sailor.

No one saw Hero and Solo and Chewy clinging together in the pocket of another sailor.

No one saw Scratcher, Morgan and Happy in a bag, thrown up aloft into the waiting arms of a sailor on the ship. Water engulfed the lifeboat and left Oleg clinging to a rope dangling from the big ship with the squealing pig clasped to his bosom and Ma's tail trailing from his wet waistcoat.

Chapter Eleven
A Pocketful of Rats

'What do we do now?' asked Hero.

In the darkness of the sailor's pocket the three baby rats clung together. The sailor had climbed on board the big new ship. He was standing on the deck, in the cold.

'Where's Ma?

'Where's Pa?'

The little rats were on their own. Now they had to make their own decisions. They listened to the sailors talking; felt their sailor shivering.

Suddenly a hand came into the pocket. A huge, thick tar-smelling, human hand with four thick fingers and a filthy thumb. Each finger was the size of one of the little rats. They stared at the hand and trembled in terror. They didn't know what to do.

Chewy bared his teeth. 'I'll bite it,' he hissed.

'Oh no! Be careful!' squeaked Hero. He wished Pa was here to tell them what to do.

'I will!' said Chewy. 'Just like Ma bit the pig.'

'Stop!' cried Hero.

He spoke too late. 'Attack!' Chewy shouted and threw himself at the hand. His claws were splayed, and his teeth suddenly, viciously, sank into the human flesh. Hero watched in horror.

'AHHHHH!' the sailor bellowed and Chewy disappeared as the sailor whipped his hand out of the pocket with the little rat still attached.

Suddenly the ship was in uproar. The sailors were whooping with a horrible laughter. Chewy bit deep into the hand. Hero and Solo looked at each other and began scrambling out of the pocket. They tumbled on to the deck and ran, zigzagging across the bare boards. Sailors thwacked the deck with ropes and lady passengers screamed and danced away in fright.

Chewy let go of the sailor's finger and went flying in an arc through the air, landing heavily in a coil of rope. In an instant he had disappeared in the coils of rope, being roughly the same dark grey colour. The sailors searched but they couldn't find him. A minute later he was but a shadow, sliding unnoticed under a cupboard door.

At the same time Solo was running across the deck. She saw a hatch and disappeared in a second into the darkness of the hold.

Hero, though, took a different course. As luck would have it, he ran through the sailors' feet, leaping and skidding and scooting across the deck. Every moment he was in grave danger – one sailor hit his tail, another stamped his big foot down in his path – but then luckily he found shelter in between some barrels and the sailors couldn't reach him.

He hid in the darkness. Next to him was a thick wooden post. Hero crouched at the bottom and looked up, way up, at the timber stretching into the sky.

It was the mast.

While the sailors were searching, Hero made his decision. Digging his claws into the wood, he began to climb the mast.

Up, up, up, he went, away from the danger below, into the realm where the canvas billowed and the taut ropes sang in the wind. He scrambled past the

yards, holding out the full-bellied sails, and continued up towards the very top of the mast. He glanced down to the deck below. He could see the sailors and the pig and other humans searching. And he saw the ocean stretching away, into a blurry horizon.

Hero climbed on. He didn't stop until quite suddenly, there was nothing more to climb. He had reached the top. Above him there was only air. He clung on by the fluttering flag and felt . . . triumphant. Excited. Frightened too. If only Pa could see him now! He had outwitted the humans! He was on top of the world. He felt exposed, but safe from the sailors. Something told him that he was different from the others who had sought the darkness. The wind made his eyes water, but it was fresh and delicious, and he gulped it down.

Chapter Twelve
An Idiotic Nest

'Chewy!' cried Pa, popping up in a far corner of the cupboard on deck. 'In here, quick! Good boy!' Pa was beaming with pleasure. Slowly the family was coming together again.

Chewy ran to Pa. There was something odd about Pa. Chewy realised he had never seen Pa smile *quite* so dazzlingly. Pa led him further back in the cupboard and into a coal scuttle. In a moment Chewy understood: Pa was covered in coal dust! His pink paws were black, his brown chin was black, his grey tail was black. And his black fur was blacker than the sootiest chimney. Only his teeth were as white as snow.

'Well done,' he said to Chewy, teeth flashing. 'This is a marvellously dirty place!' he boasted, as they went in. 'Quite filthy! Come in. Your mother and some of your brothers and sisters are here. It will make a tremendous nest, while we gather our wits together.'

Chewy was relieved to be back with the family. Pa led the way deeper into the coal scuttle. 'Ma, I've found Chewy,' he said to a piece of coal.

'I'm here,' replied Ma, behind him.

'So you are,' said Pa. 'It is terrifically dark in here.'

'Chewy, Chewy,' came a series of little cries.

Chewy found the rats all snuggled together in the coal. He told them of his escape with Hero and Solo. Ma was so grateful that all her little rats had made it.

'We'll have to send out search parties for them,' she told Pa, 'after dark, when it is safe. Who knows what danger they are in.'

'Shhh!'

The rats fell silent. Someone was at the entrance to the coal scuttle. Pa bared his teeth.

'Hellooooo?' a little voice called down to them.

The rats didn't move.

'Anybody. There?' called the voice. It was another rat.

Pa decided that it was his duty to protect and speak for his family. Whatever the danger.

'I. Am. Here,' he called back in what he hoped was a very firm, very authoritative voice.

'Who – Am – "I"?' said the voice, sounding a little perplexed, but trying to be equally firm and authoritative.

Pa paused. 'I don't know,' he replied, not really prepared for this guessing game. 'Who *are* you?'

There was a further pause.

'I mean – Who Are *You*?' said the voice, correcting itself.

Pa was confused. He felt it was wrong for this intruder to demand who *he* was, without first identifying herself. He was convinced that it was a 'herself' now, because it was such a small, frail voice. He thought she must be a rather stupid rat. 'Who are you?'

'I asked first,' persisted the voice.

'So what?' cried Pa, stamping his foot now.

The other rat thought for a moment. 'I am Marion,' she said at last. 'The oldest resident on the ship. Now – who are you?'

'Rufus,' said Pa. Was that a small victory he had just won, he wondered. He wasn't sure.

'What are you doing in a coal scuttle?' asked Marion, coming down towards them. She blinked as she peered into the darkness.

'Well,' began Pa, curling his tail uncertainly, 'it is our nest.'

'Nest?' hooted Marion. 'There are few enough rats on board, without having some who want to end their days in a fire! Oh, my goodness!' she squeaked excitedly. 'There are *lots* of you. A family! Oh, how lovely! A little *young* family! We haven't had one of those on board for *ages!*'

'Oh, ha-ha. Yes. We are a young family,' admitted Pa, flushing with pleasure, and beaming broadly once again.

'How nice to meet you,' said Ma, remembering her manners; and feeling sure that this old rat would be helpful to them, she came forward a few steps.

'But you are such an *idiotic* family,' said the old rat, blinking benignly.

Pa's smile froze on his face. Ma's whiskers bristled. The little rats giggled as they took this splendid insult in.

'S . . . sorry?' said Pa and Ma together.

'If you make your home in a coal scuttle,' Marion explained, 'Spurdle, the cook, will throw you on his fire, with the coal! How perfectly *idiotic* of you.'

Pa twitched. His snout rose in the air. 'It was only temporary accommodation,' he informed her coldly. 'We are in hiding.'

'We weren't making a nest *here*!' Ma told the old rat. 'You didn't think that, did you? '

'Oh, good,' said Marion, 'because I can show you something *much* better. Hello, little ones! Welcome on board. Follow Auntie Marion.'

Chapter Thirteen
Beautiful Blossom

As the stars came out above, and the moon rose glittering over the silver sea, Hero found himself hungry beyond belief. There wasn't a morsel of food to be had up there on top of the mast. Not a gnat. As the darkness fell, he decided he had to venture down.

So, leaving his splendid position, he gripped a rope with his claws and picked his way carefully down to the deck below.

All was quiet. Two sailors stood at the stern guiding the ship through the water. Another sat on a chest near the bows, huddled in a coat.

A hatch opened and a man came out carrying a

bucket. It was the ship's cook, Spurdle. The smell of vegetable peelings made Hero lick his lips and, keeping to the shadows, he eagerly followed the man.

Spurdle headed straight for a temporary hut erected on the starboard side of the deck. He crouched down at the doorway and put the bucket inside. 'There you are, Pork Scratching,' he chuckled. 'Fatten you up a little, eh?' There was an excited snuffling and snorting noise from the pig. ''Ungry, are you?' chuckled Spurdle.

'Hungry, of course she is,' declared Oleg Olegovitch. His head popped up from the sty.

''Cripes, it's you,' said Spurdle, banging his head on the door jamb. 'Ow.'

'Thank you for this fine pig food,' Oleg said.

Spurdle studied the Russian captain. 'What are you doing here?'

'I sleep with Blossom. I am protection.'

'You *sleep* with that pig?' exclaimed Spurdle, curling his lip. 'Disgusting.' He spat.

Hero crept closer. He found a dropped potato peeling and ate it quickly.

'Yes. It is smelly. But this pig precious,' Oleg declared.

'This pig . . . tasty,' replied Spurdle, mimicking the captain's speech. 'This pig will make a good roast supper.' He smacked his lips. 'We are going to enjoy this pig. Trotters and all. Captain McNeeps has already inquired about apple sauce and crackling!' he laughed.

'This my pig! No one eat my pig,' hissed Oleg. He stepped out of the sty and stood towering over the spindly cook. 'No one! You hear me? I have nothing left in the world. No money. Nothing. Only Blossom.'

Spurdle shrank away from the captain. 'Yeah. We'll see,' he muttered darkly, as he left.

Nearby, Hero was hastily nibbling a mouldy cheese rind and half a potato. How nicely the humans treated the pig, he thought. He wondered why. He was also thankful to the pig as his stomach was happily filling up on scraps that Blossom was spraying around the deck.

Oleg patted the pig. 'Steady, Bloss. You eat. Eat as much as you want. Get nice and fat, Bloss,' he said. 'This ship rich, Bloss. They got lots of money. And you like to help your master, eh, Bloss? After all the things I done for you? One day I get back to Murmansk. I tell them all about you, Bloss.

Someday I get back.' He took out a mouth harp, and putting it to his lips, began to play a Russian tune that reminded him of home.

Hero paused in his eating. The sound that Oleg made with the little instrument – a strange and wonderful twanging – made his fur stand on end. Hero stood still and listened. The music was so sweet, it made his head swim with wondrous dreams. He felt soothed and inspired at the same time. Music was a fine thing, he thought, and with shining eyes he gazed admiringly at the huge human who played it.

But as Hero lingered, transfixed by the music, and the stars twinkled above him, the silhouette of another animal picked its way along the side of the boat . . .

Chapter Fourteen
The Best Nest

'The ship is heading south!' Pa did a little dance when Marion told him. He rushed up and nuzzled Ma. Together they shook their bottoms in happiness.

'We are leaving the cold behind! We are going to the Tropics, where it's hot and steamy, and there ain't no snow! Now we must find a nest, the best nest — and everything will be well. We sit tight, we lie back . . . Time passes . . . and we reach our destination.'

'You are clever, Pa,' said Morgan.

'Luck, my boy. Good luck. Never underestimate the importance of Luck in your life. Seek it out.

Give it a little tickle!' Pa beamed.

The little family scurried along the rat runs between the decks. Marion, then Pa (whistling lightly through his teeth), then the little ones, then Ma. Suddenly Marion stopped. Above them they heard a noise.

Purrrrrrrrr-Purrrrrrrr

Purrrrrrrrr-Purrrrrrrr

'We are under the galley,' Marion whispered. 'And that is Menace.' Her little eyes narrowed with hatred. 'That cat is a cold-hearted, ruthless killer!'

'Does she want to eat us?" asked Happy.

Marion nodded and addressed the little rats directly. 'I have never met a meaner cat. She lives for only one thing: to make this ship free of rats. That is her mission in life. She cares for nothing else. She is everywhere. Sniffing and stalking and listening – oh!' Marion shuddered and cried out. 'Menace has killed all my rats! Every one of them. She has killed all my dear children, and so many of my dear friends. Little ones – I have only one piece of advice – stay away from Menace. She is looking for you every second of every hour of every day.'

'Come on now – don't frighten them,' Ma said. 'We are safe here and we're going to find a new nest, so let's be merry and bright.'

The rats crept under the wooden boards, away from the purring cat. Marion sighed.

'Very well, there are two possibilities,' she said, her eyes rekindling with their little twinkle. 'First there is the powder room at the end of the gun deck. It is very safe, because the sailors don't go in there. But you will have to find all your own nesting materials. It is a little bare.'

'Bare is good for us,' said Pa, sticking his snout in the air and putting on a decisive military air. 'It will make us hardy. I like the powder room.'

Ma coughed. 'Not so hasty. Where is the other place?' she enquired.

'Just here.' Marion smiled at Ma, and disappeared down a chute to a lower deck. Everyone followed one after the other, the little rats squealing happily. They landed in a heap in the hold, surrounded by packing cases.

Marion smiled indulgently at the little rats tumbling around. 'Aren't they sweet.' She nudged Pa. 'I just love to see babies again.'

'Um,' Pa agreed. They were sweet, but they were also his responsibility. Somehow that made them less sweet.

'Here is a very desirable tea chest,' said Marion. 'One entrance, plenty of straw. Inside there's a marble human head for company.'

'No, no,' Ma objected. 'The head would give me the creeps.'

'Or there's this – a long crate with a thing called a canoe in it.'

Ma shook her head.

'Or here, my favourite – this is a *special* nest: a lidless chest, containing a china tea service, packed in straw with two entrances, a biscuit barrel, and eight teacups, all in beautiful blue and white Chinese willow pattern. Isn't that a nice nest? The kids could each have a cup to sleep in!'

'Oh, yes, yes!' the little rats cried.

'Can we?' Ma turned to Pa, smiling.

Pa considered. 'Could I sleep in the teapot?' he asked.

'If I can have the biscuit barrel,' laughed Ma.

'Good. This is it,' declared Pa. 'Here is our new nest. Enjoy it. Treasure it. Make yourself at home,' he told them, behaving as if he were a guest of honour opening a village fête.

The little ones needed no encouragement. They dived into the nest and kicked straw at each other.

They burrowed down to the very bottom of the tea chest and reappeared with silver spoons and sugar tongs. Which they threw at each other. They played hide-and-seek among the cups, saucers and the hot-water jug. They broke the milk jug. Scratcher tunnelled through to a neighbouring crate full of sea sponges and horsehair cushions and Morgan got lost in there. And then they threw sponges at each other. Happy kicked bundles of straw over the edge of the chest and watched them fall to the deck.

'Aren't they sweet?' said Pa flatly.

'I must be going,' said Marion, dazed by this behaviour. She set off through the packing cases.

'Pa!'

Pa glanced up. The cases were stacked above him, like towers in a city of boxes. Someone up there was calling him.

'Pa!'

Pa couldn't see them. One of the children, obviously.

'Come down from up there,' he ordered. 'At once, before . . .'

There was a screech and a small thing landed on him. It was a rat. Pa finished his sentence beneath the small thing. 'Before you fall and hurt

yourself or . . .'

'Solo,' cried Ma, rushing up. 'Darling — where have you been?'

'Or fall and hurt *me*,' Pa muttered. 'Solo, get off.'

'Yes, Pa. Sorry, Pa.' Solo smiled broadly. 'I slipped.'

'Where's your brother?' asked Ma, nuzzling her.

'I don't know,' said Solo. She looked down at the floor. 'I was chased by the humans and then I met a cat and I hid from it. And Hero disappeared. And I don't know where he went. I called and I called, but he didn't answer. He may be up there still, or he may be . . .' Solo shuddered.

'Oh, my Hero — my little one with the twitchy paws!' cried Ma, upset. 'I hope he has not been eaten by that cat, Menace. Being eaten by a cat would be horrid!' She looked at Pa.

'Quite horrid,' Pa assured her. 'I shall go out tonight,' he declared. 'I shall search the ship for the little fellow, and bring him back safe and sound.'

'Oh, you are wonderful,' said Ma admiringly.

'Unless, of course, he's been eaten,' added Pa, realising that his boast might be a bit rash.

Chapter Fifteen
Jim

Hero lay flat in the shadow of the moon by Blossom's sty. His fur bristled. The magical twanging music from the mouth harp faded. The cat was stalking the deck. She was coming towards him. Hero knew he must stay as still as a stone. But he was ready to run.

This is what it felt like to be hunted. To be ready to spring and fight or spring and flee . . . or lie low and hope the hunter passed you by. Hero tried to imagine that he didn't exist, and if that happened then the cat would pass him by.

The wind moved lightly across the deck, lifting his whiskers. The cat stopped. The cat crouched.

Hero's heart was in his mouth. *Run*, his limbs seemed to shout. He could see the cat's muscles tense beneath the fur . . .

'Look, Blossom, pussy cat come,' said Oleg. He stretched out a hand and rubbed his thumb and forefinger together. 'Her name is Menace, Blossom. She is a rat-catcher.'

Menace looked at Oleg and the pig. She seemed to be thinking of something else. Her ears were pricked in a different direction.

As Menace rose, Hero sprang. He fled from the cat across the deck. But with a *yowl*, Menace leaped upon Hero. She caught his tail, swiping with her deadly claws, missed and turned, missed again, and Hero ran free – almost to the other side of the deck and safety. In two great leaps the cat was on top of Hero, hissing and biting the air as Hero twisted out of the way and ran again. Once more Menace sprang and sank her teeth into his back – but not firmly enough and Hero had found a hole in the deck. As Menace opened her mouth to bite more firmly, Hero twisted into the hole.

He lay there, trembling. Menace breathed through the hole, spitting and biting the air in frustration. Hero moved away. He was in a rat run beneath the deck and he thankfully squirmed into the darkness, panting with relief.

Humans, pigs and cats, he thought. *The humans are kind to the pigs and to the cats. But why are they all enemies of the rat?*

Hero slept. The exhaustion of the chase and the fear that had gripped him had tired him out. He curled up in a corner and nursed his wounds. They weren't too bad. But the cat had a taste for him now and they were deadly enemies.

So be it, thought Hero. *I must be brave. I must keep going. For the time being, I am alive, and that is what counts. Now I must seek out my family.* He sniffed the air in an attempt to lift his spirits and set off through the ship.

After a while he came to a hole in the floor of the rat run. Beyond it he could see a light and he peeped over the edge.

He was above the sailors' sleeping quarters. Immediately below the hole lay a hammock, and the face of a human – a boy. The boy saw Hero, saw the rat's little black eye and the pink quivering snout, and his eyes lit up with interest.

Hero froze. He stared back at the boy and prepared to run. He knew he must be wary of humans. And yet the boy's eyes were fascinating. He didn't look like a hunter, not like the cat, Menace . . .

The boy's hand came towards Hero. All Hero's senses began screaming, *Flee, run, don't touch!* But, Hero stayed rooted to the spot. Up came the boy's hand, towards the hole, into the hole, and Hero smelled . . . a raisin.

Hero couldn't resist the raisin. He longed for that sweet taste. His mouth watered. He would risk the danger. He thrust his head forward, nibbled at the raisin and then swiftly plucked it from the boy's fingers, and ate it.

Deeeeeelicious!

The boy laughed softly. Held up another one. Hero took it.

Hero allowed the boy's finger to come close. He sniffed the finger. Tar. Pine. Grime. Raisin. He could bite it! – No! he mustn't! He remembered what had happened to Chewy, who had been flung across the deck. Hero trembled with confusion.

The boy's finger came through the hole . . . the finger stroked Hero's head and his coat . . . Hero didn't like it. It was . . . frightening . . . but then, if he relaxed, he found that it was in fact . . . nice. Tingles of pleasure ran down his back. The boy's finger was gentle and sensitive.

What am I doing? Hero thought, his eyes closing as he abandoned himself to this pleasure. This is a human and humans are full of hatred for us. He could almost hear Pa's outrage!

And yet . . .

He was unable to drag himself away. He felt the pleasure of submitting to the caress of the boy. After a while, he opened his eyes and craned his neck to study the boy. He saw curly dark hair and brown eyes and this great big hand, stroking, stroking, stroking him.

'Hello, little rat,' whispered the boy. His mouth cracked into a crooked grin. 'My name is Jim.' But Hero didn't understand human language. He only knew the words were kind.

He felt that he had been put under a spell, and it was only with difficulty that he pulled himself away and scuttled off, away from the hole above the boy's hammock, breathing hard, and wondering at the significance of what had just happened.

Chapter Sixteen
Reunited

Hero roamed the ship looking for food and his family. Both were important, but he found himself thinking about food more than family. It was a case of the stomach ruling the heart. He left the rat run above the sailors' quarters and found a way down into the hold. Here he was surrounded by packing cases stacked one on top of the other.

Running along between them, he smelled something good. Something vegetably and wet: potato peelings! He rushed round the corner towards the smell – only to find that another, bigger rat was already there.

Hero watched the big rat scoffing the potato

peelings, while at the same time dragging a paper bag full of the peelings behind him.

What a greedy rat! He obviously wanted it all for himself. There must be some way Hero could eat some of the peelings. He was suddenly desperate with hunger. Hero crept up, hoping a peeling might be left behind for him. Suddenly the big rat spun round, hissing.

'Get off! . . . AH, OH!' It was Pa.

'Pa!' shrieked Hero.

'Hero! – you sneaky rat! Hello, darling! Where have you been? Help me with this, it is so awkward!'

'Can I eat one . . .'

'Of course – the more you eat the less we have to carry. I am on my way back to the little ones. They are close by. Just wait till Ma sees you. She will be *so* pleased. Ma! Ma!' he called as Hero began to eat.

'My Hero!' shrieked Ma, running towards them.

'Potato peels! Potato peels!' cried the little ones and they mobbed Hero and fell upon the potato peelings.

The family settled down into the new nest in the tea chest full of straw and china. Pa took the teapot, Ma the biscuit barrel; the little rats each had a teacup. Everything was back to normal.

Pa enjoyed singing through the spout.

'We are a family again,' he told them. His voice echoed strangely. 'Luck is with us: we are on a grand ship. We are on our way to the Tropics. To the lands of heat and spice and sleepy lagoons. My thought for the day is this: life is what you make of it!' (The little rats giggled in their teacups.) 'If you laze around, sitting in teacups all day long, and never explore, then your life will be poor and unfulfilled. Little ones, you are growing up, you are changing. Venture Forth, Enjoy Freedom and Experience Life: live it to the Full. Breathe in the foul and fetid air. Seek out the deliciously filthy. Discover the dank and the rank – and wallow, wallow in it, children! Right now I am going to have a bath in the bilge water.'

The little rats imagined the dank and the rank, the foul and the fetid and the deliciously filthy, and they made up their minds to Experience It.

Then Ma spoke from the biscuit barrel: 'Please, darlings, *beware* of the ship's cat, Menace, she is after us day and night, slinking in the shadows. *Beware* of the cook too; Spurdle is his name, for he is sure to be a dab hand at catching rats and popping them in his big black pot. And *beware* of the cannons on the gun deck, for if you crawl in there and fall asleep, you may be blasted out clinging to a cannonball.'

That would be exciting, the little ones giggled, as they trooped off to join Pa for a dark and smelly bath in the bilges.

Hero didn't feel like a bath in the bilges. He was happy lying in his teacup with his tail wrapped around the twirly handle. He was thinking.

He loved his family. They had been so pleased to see him. He had told them all about his adventures. But every time that he said something that they didn't like or agree with, they told him so, loudly and forcefully.

He had said that he liked music – and they had told him how *HORRIBLE* music was. How it set their teeth on edge and made their fur stand on end and their whiskers twitch uncontrollably. He said he had met a boy who had given him a raisin – and they had said it was *FOUL* to be near such a hideous enemy.

He didn't dare tell them that the boy Jim had stroked him. And spoken kindly to him. He knew exactly what their reaction would have been.

Hero lay in the teacup looking up at all the packing cases around him. He felt hungry again. He was growing and the potato peelings were long gone.

He thought of the boy and the raisin (in fact he thought of the raisin and *then* the boy) and he decided to set off and find him. Now he knew where the family was nesting, he could come back anytime.

It was evening when Hero found the boy's hammock, and it was empty. He gazed down at the gently swaying canvas and at the bundle of clothes on it. He sniffed the air. He *could* smell raisins! Did the boy keep raisins?

Remembering Pa's advice to Venture Forth and Experience Life, Hero jumped easily through the hole and dropped on to the hammock.

There were definitely raisins here. He could smell them. The raisins were hidden in a rolled-up shirt. Hero tore a hole in the shirt, and took out ten sweet raisins. Crouching in the murky light of the sleeping quarters, he ate them all. Then, satisfied, he curled up under the shirt. Just for a moment.

He closed his eyes and listened to the wash of water, and the sharp crying of the seagulls and the far–off *ding-ding-ding-ding* of the ship's bell. As they sailed south, the air was warming up. The sea wind had lost its chill and a balmy breeze was wafting gently through the ship.

Hero began to dream. He liked the warm salt air. He liked the feel of the boy's linen shirt. And soon he fell asleep.

He woke with a start: someone was climbing in! The little rat tensed, ready to spring. The human froze. It was the boy, Jim. *He's seen me,* Hero thought, his eyes wide and alert. His tail was sticking out. Idiot rat! Hero could only wait as, very slowly, the boy Jim lifted the corner of the shirt.

Hero lay exposed.

Help! Hero's little voice rang in his head. *Help!* His limbs quivered. Something held him back, a feeling perhaps, a memory of the fingers that stroked so gently . . .

Very slowly, Jim found a raisin and held it out to the little rat.

Hero smelled it. Then he saw it. *Be brave*, he told himself. He took the raisin in his paw.

Jim found a biscuit.

Hero thought, *I like this boy.* Hero ate the biscuit. And as he ate, Jim climbed in.

And Hero stayed, in the crook of the boy's arm.

And so the cabin boy, Jim, and the little rat Hero, became friends. Hero began to change. He visited Jim every day and was given bits of food. And every time he secretly celebrated his craftiness. What a clever way to find food! What a clever, crafty rat he was.

But he didn't tell his family. He knew that they would not approve. Making friends with the enemy – just imagine the lecture from Pa!

One evening Hero listened as Jim whispered him his story – of how he ran away to sea to escape from his father. How his father was a tailor and Jim was made to mend sails all day and sew buttons on Captain McNeeps' uniform. He could sew fantastically well, and all the sailors brought him their clothes to mend and patch.

Hero didn't understand the boy and his talk, but he could understand the tone of voice. Jim talked to him in kind whispers, like Oleg talked to Blossom – like a secret, adoring friend. The tone made Hero feel warm and soft inside.

For the next week Hero watched the humans

whenever he could. While the rest of the family were below decks, sniffing through the cargo, hunting cockroaches and rubbish, or bathing in the dirty bilge water, Hero studied the humans.

They were dancing the hornpipe, eating with knives and forks, reading books, looking through telescopes, climbing up the rigging, singing sea shanties as they worked. Privately, Hero did his own little dances this way and that – sometimes even rearing up on his hind legs before toppling down. At night, when he occasionally curled up with Jim, he imagined what it would be like to be a human, to wear clothes and sing and have nice manners and be so very big.

Wouldn't it be grand?

Chapter Seventeeen
Afternoon Tea

One day, as Ma and Pa and the little ones snoozed in their nest of china, they had a visitor. They had just enjoyed a long and delicious lunch of discarded fish heads and potatoes. Pa was snoring, whistling through his teeth as he dreamed of pungent dustbins. Ma was licking her lips, as she dreamed of cream buns. The children were flat out, dreaming that they were tumbling down mountains of sifted white sugar.

At teatime the hatch opened, and Spurdle the cook climbed down the ladder into the hold.

'Here you are, Menace,' Spurdle muttered. 'There's a few vermin in here, I shouldn't wonder.'

'Quick,' cried Ma, waking up instantly. 'Into the biscuit barrel!'

Hero, Chewy, Happy, Solo and Scratcher tumbled out of their teacups and squeezed into the biscuit barrel, pulling the lid over them. Ma and Pa and Morgan sat in the teapot and listened.

'Are we hiding here?' asked Morgan. His tail twitched nervously.

'Un-for-tunately,' said Pa slowly. He could hear Spurdle approaching, moving boxes. He remembered Marion's warning about the cook and shuddered. Ma looked at Pa, her eyes wide in alarm. The man was coming closer.

'This is another stupid nest,' growled Pa through gritted teeth. He banged his head on the side of the teapot.

'Why's it stupid?' asked Morgan.

'Because there's no escape,' hissed Pa, his eyes popping with frustration. 'I am an idiot!'

'Here it is,' said the cook, right on top of the little rats now, and suddenly he reached in and lifted up the teapot out of the straw in the chest! Horrified, Ma, Pa and Morgan teetered, scrabbled then fell around inside. Spurdle placed the teapot on a tray. He didn't remove the lid. The rats lay there in the dark, trembling.

Now they heard the other parts of the tea service being picked out and placed on the tray – first cups, then jugs, and then the biscuit barrel.

'Oh dear,' Ma fretted. 'Oh dear, oh dear.' She twisted her whiskers in her mouth and nibbled her paws and scampered fast round and round the teapot.

'Calm yourself,' Pa hissed through gritted teeth. 'Stay still.'

'Idiot rat,' he told himself, and hit his forehead. 'Ow.'

Morgan watched his parents with concern.

Ma stopped running. Pa stopped hitting his forehead. They bristled. A throbbing noise was outside the teapot, a deadly purring, coming closer all the time – the cat was exploring the tea service.

A green eye appeared at the top of the spout.

The cat blinked down at the trapped rats. Pa bared his teeth. The purring rang round the walls of the teapot. The cat couldn't reach them. Pa shut his eyes.

Prepare to run, he thought, and his mind turned again to puddings. The image of a lemon tart swam before him. If he had a last request before being eaten, lemon tart would be a good choice – with cream and a little light pastry.

'Miaoooooowwwww!' Menace bawled.

'Geddorf,' cried Spurdle. He pushed the cat away and a moment later the tray was lifted up and the little rats' stomachs flipped over. Spurdle carried the tea service up the ladder and out of the hold.

The rats clung to each other.

A few minutes later they were on the table in the galley. Spurdle disappeared into the stores.

Pa and Ma and Morgan pushed off the teapot lid and scrambled out as quickly as they could. Pa peeped in the biscuit barrel.

Cowering at the bottom were Hero, Scratcher, Solo, Chewy and Happy. Quick as a flash, Ma and Morgan jumped in.

'You can't hide there –' began Pa.

But Spurdle was coming back. Pa had a choice: he could jump from the table and run for it and save his skin (and enjoy pudding again) or he could stick with his family.

He jumped . . . into the biscuit barrel, into the arms of his family, and quickly pulled the lid over them all, as if it were the cover to a drain in the street of a big city. He burrowed down into the darkness, into the warmth of the seven other rats.

'When he opens the lid,' Pa whispered, 'everyone *run*. Run for your lives, run helter-skelter, in different directions, all over the place. Understand?'

'Yes, Pa,' squeaked the little rats.

Pa felt seven little hearts around him beating fast. They all listened to the clinking of china. To the rattle of spoons. The whistle of the kettle. The hollow slooshing of hot water filling the teapot . . . and sooner or later . . .

But the cook never looked inside the biscuit barrel. Instead the tray — together with the teapot and the biscuit barrel — was lifted up and carried through the ship. On and on, for what seemed like ages, until they were put down again.

'Where are we?' whispered Hero directly into Pa's ear.

'I have no idea,' replied Pa darkly.

'My nerves,' wailed Ma.

Outside they could hear voices. The rats listened. It was Captain McNeeps with some lady passengers. The captain was a big man with a long red beard and he spoke in a soft Scottish voice, full of a quiet authority. The ritual of tea was beginning.

'Ahh, tea! Thank you, cook.'

'A welcome sight.'

'Biscuits too,' twittered a high voice.

Only a matter of time, thought Pa, bracing himself. He listened to further clinking and pouring.

'Sugar?'

'Ummm.'

'Biscuits?'

The biscuit barrel was picked up. Eight terrified rats prepared to jump. The lid was taken off. The rats were presented.

'OOOOOOOOOH! AAAAAAAAAHHH! EEEEEERRRRRRGGGGGHHHHHH!

The screams that followed – the whooping, hysterical, gargling screeches – would ring in the rats' ears for many months after. Captain McNeeps himself presented the biscuit barrel full of rats and when he saw them, he dropped it on his toe and leaped about the cabin before finding an umbrella and bashing the floor madly.

Two ladies fainted. Another stood on a chair and screamed.

'Quick – run!' bellowed Ma.

The little rats ran.

Here-there-everywhere. Across the cabin. Into the bed. Over the charts, up the curtains, bumping into the wall and back again.

'Escape!' cried Pa, running round in circles.

Captain McNeeps stabbed the floor energetically with the umbrella. 'Ha ha ha!' he cried, like a demented clown.

'Go under the bed,' shrieked Solo, seeing a hole in the floor.

McNeeps shouted for help.

The door opened and Menace bounded in. She was followed by Spurdle. Straightaway Menace caught Scratcher with a terrible blow on the head and, sadly, very sadly, that was the end of her.

'Brute,' cried Pa, blood boiling and whiskers bristling.

Ma ran to Scratcher. She touched Scratcher's face, and saw that she was lifeless and then Ma raged against the world and every cat in it. 'You'll pay for this!' she screamed as she dodged McNeeps' umbrella. She would have fought Menace there and then – but she had a family to think of.

'In here, in here,' urged Hero. The rats were running under the bed, and Ma ran with them, but suddenly the cook loomed over Hero, with a carving knife in his hand and cut him off from his family. In the pandemonium that followed, Hero did an unusual thing.

He ran *towards* the cook. He ran over his shoe. He ran *up his trouser leg.*

Spurdle dropped the knife and clutched his leg in horror. He lurched out of the cabin, baying, 'RRRRAAAAAAATTTTTTTT! I've a RAAAAAAAAT in ME PANTS! Help me, OOOOh.'

It was not nice for Spurdle. It was not nice for Hero either. Rat and human were not mixing happily – but the rat's bravery was winning out.

Leaping up the gangway, Spurdle lurched out on to the deck, where he began tearing at his buttons, desperately wrenching his trousers off.

Two sailors ran to him – but instead of helping, they collapsed in laughter! Hero's claws were sharp and the cook's face was contorted in horror.

At last Hero jumped free, scrambling out of the back of the cook's trousers, leaping straight into the pig's pen, the nearest place of cover. Blossom the pig snorted, shrieked and squealed. Spurdle sank to his knees. Oleg, who saw the little furry shadow tumble into his beloved pig's pen, shouted and pointed: 'There he is! Disgustink RRRRRat!'

And then the sailors were after him. Hero hid; he

burrowed into the pig's rubbish. He squirmed deep down into it, hiding from the crowd that wanted to capture him. Too late he realised that he had backed himself into a corner. A sailor was looming over him. He looked up, certain that he was about to meet his end – and looked – straight into a face that he recognised.

Jim!

'Here, boy, I'll look after you,' Jim whispered urgently. He held open his pocket. Hero, trembling dreadfully, and hardly thinking straight, scampered quickly in.

'It's gone,' the boy announced to the crew. 'Gone down a hole.'

The sailors laughed. 'Good luck to it,' said someone.

Only Spurdle wasn't laughing. Clutching his bottom, he swore revenge.

Chapter Eighteen

A Dish Served Cold

'Revenge' said Pa, swimming in the bilges with an old cigar butt in his mouth. (It was deliciously disgusting.) 'Revenge is the only course.'

'Revenge?' queried Chewy.

'That's it. Hero and Scratcher are dead. Killed by that vile cook and his cat. We must seek revenge. We must punish them. If we don't punish them – who will?'

Ma tut-tutted, and wiped her whiskers. 'I said "beware". I did. It doesn't matter that I should expect to lose one or two of the babies on such a perilous journey – it still hurts. I loved that little rat, Hero. He had those twitchy paws. And a lovely white spot on his belly. And I loved Scratcher too. She was all fire – up for anything. I'll always remember her fidgeting in the nest. She could never keep still.'

'It's the cook, Pa, I saw the cook got Hero,' Morgan said.

'I know,' said Pa. 'He was a hero to the last – running into the cook's drawers to save his family.'

'We should cook the cook,' said Happy.

'We should destroy his kitchen,' said Chewy, munching on the sole of an old shoe.

Pa gazed at his offspring. What fine rats they were! They showed loyalty. And spirit! And they were commendably filthy. He felt proud to be their father. 'It is a fine and noble idea to cook the cook – but too ambitious. I have another idea. Chewy, now that it is dark and all the sailors are asleep, I'd like you to come with me. You and I and your wonderful teeth have a job to do.'

Pa took Chewy through the dark ship to the sailors' sleeping quarters, stopping now and then to sniff the air for a sign of Menace. He climbed on to a trunk and up a bunk followed by Chewy and together they slipped carefully around a snoring sailor. At the top of the bunk, Pa pointed to a near-by hammock.

'There's the villain Spurdle,' he whispered, his black eyes narrowing wickedly. 'Time for a little mischief . . .'

Chewy didn't need any encouragement. He scrambled on to a nearby shelf and leaped on to one end of the hammock. It shook gently. He climbed up and began to chew the rope that held the sleeping Spurdle. While the cook dreamed of catching rats and putting them on trial, Chewy chomped through the rope until with a sudden TWANG! the rope holding the hammock gave way.

Oh joy!

Spurdle plummeted to the deck – there was an awful THUMP! as he landed, which was quickly followed by a scream of pain and anger. Pa crouched on the bunk laughing merrily. Chewy fell with the hammock and ran off into the darkness. One of the disturbed sailors held a lantern up. 'What's goin' on?'

'Filthy vermin!' screamed Spurdle, rubbing his back. 'Chewed me hammock off!'

Someone turned up an oil lamp. Across the room Pa saw Ma, on her hind legs, with her front paws

held out like a boxing kangaroo. 'You disgusting man!' she shouted. 'That's what you get for killing my babies!' With a snarl, she turned and disappeared.

Pa was surprised to see Ma – though he guessed that she knew him well enough to read his mind – but he was even *more* surprised to see Hero. The little rat was on the other side of the room, sitting up in a hammock, wearing . . . wearing . . . Pa blinked and rubbed his eyes. He couldn't believe . . . Rats do have poor eyesight, it is true, but Pa could have *sworn* that it was Hero . . . and he was wearing a *spotty handkerchief*!

Chapter Nineteen
Saviour and Protector

After his escape from Spurdle's trousers, Hero had stayed hidden in Jim's pocket. He was carried all over the ship, in the pocket. It was safe there and Jim looked after him. In the early evening he took Hero up to the crow's nest, high up above the ship, in the fresh air and warm sunshine. After the hair-raising chase from the captain's cabin, Hero felt so happy to be alive.

There were good humans and bad humans, he realised. But how did you tell one from the other?

Jim gave him bread and a tiny piece of cheese. Hero let himself be washed and stroked as Jim talked to him. Hero liked the boy, his saviour and

119

protector, and let the boy look after him.

And it was nice for Jim too. Jim wanted Hero to be his pet. A pet he could talk to and play with during the long hours at sea. When night came, Jim took Hero out of his pocket and washed him with soap and hid him in his hammock. He made a tiny bed of clean linen sheets for Hero. He cut a strip from his red spotty handkerchief and tied it around Hero's neck.

Hero was his rat now. Wasn't he?

'Never trust your eyes,' said Pa, trying to get comfortable in their temporary nest in a box of rags on the gun deck. 'Use your nose for smelling, your ears for hearing and your whiskers for feeling. But never trust your eyes.'

'Why's that?' asked Happy.

'Because with my eyes I thought I saw Hero, sitting in a sailor's hammock,' said Pa.

'Really?' said Ma. 'Oh, how exciting! He's not dead after all.'

'The thing is,' said Pa slowly, 'he was wearing a little red spotted handkerchief round his neck.'

There was silence. The rats considered it very peculiar to have a handkerchief round your neck.

'It's been a long night,' Ma told Pa gently, 'and you have had a lot of excitement.'

'Never trust your eyes,' Pa repeated and closed them for a sleep.

In the morning, Solo appeared. She had been out all night, scavenging.

'I was on the poop deck,' she told them, 'in the early morning, and I saw Hero. He was with the boy. The thing is, he was wearing a handkerchief – like you said – around his neck, and . . . a thing like a coat.'

'A *coat*?' exclaimed Pa.

'In this weather?' said Ma.

'A *coat*?' repeated Pa. 'Are you sure?'

'I'm sure. It has a silvery swirl pattern. And little holes for his front paws.'

'At least he is alive. But it is jolly hot for a coat,' said Ma, frowning. 'And he has lovely fur.'

Ma and Pa didn't know what to make of it. It took one of the little ones to sum up all their feelings. Morgan spoke slowly:

'But Hero is a rat, Ma. He isn't a human, is he?'

'Exactly.' Pa nodded sagely. 'He doesn't need a coat. Nature has already given him one. It would appear that our Hero has become confused. If you ask me, he has a strange idea of appropriate rat behaviour! If he is a rat – he must stay a rat! After all, you are what you are. You are not what you are not. And he is not . . . a human!'

'Whatever next?' wondered Ma.

Chapter Twenty
Hero the Human

'He is wearing *trousers*!' squealed Happy.

'And a *hat*!' said Chewy.

'And he has a little sword!' chimed Morgan.

Ma and Pa stuck their heads out from behind a barrel. A week had passed and they were living in a warm, dry storeroom on the gun deck. (Pa had chosen it. After the episode with the tea service he didn't want any more suggestions from Marion. 'Just wait till I see her – I shall tell her exactly how *special* her last nest was . . .' he grumbled.)

But news of Hero's transformation worried Ma and Pa and they spent a lot of time in conference, wondering what to do and trying to keep their worry from the little ones.

'Enough,' said Pa, in the end, 'I am going to speak with him.'

It was dawn and Pa set off in the direction of the poop deck where Hero had last been seen with the boy. He ran along the gun deck, from cannon to cannon, pausing occasionally to sniff the air. Passing the galley, he caught sight of Menace asleep and paused. If he could only bite that twitching tail . . . but no, it would have to be something bigger – something more final to get back at that cat.

He paused by the stairs, sniffed, then quickly scuttled up the steps to the poop deck. He took cover behind a mast and listened. He could hear the boy! He was nearby. Speaking softly – his voice was full of excitement.

'That's it. Parry, parry, lunge! Withdraw – now – feint – and lunge! Hey, you are good! Good Rocco. Good rat, Rocco! Are you tired? Eh? Very well. You go down on your front paws – I gotta check the lines, then we'll practise some more.'

Pa heard the boy moving to the back of the ship. He looked round the mast and what he saw made him gasp. His front legs buckled in amazement.

There was Hero, in a silvery jacket. On his head

there was a fancy floppy hat with a *feather* in it – and boots – tiny black leather *boots*. And a tiddly sword, the size of a needle.

What did he think he was doing? Who did he think he was? Some prancing rat-cavalier? Pa shook with outrage.

'R–r–r–r–r–r–Rocco?' he hissed, imitating the sound that the boy made.

Hero twitched. His eyes swivelled.

'R–r–r–r–r–r–Rocco?'

Hero spun round and saw Pa. His body jolted upright and he rose up on his hind legs and held the sword out.

Pa fought to control his anger.

'Hero, what do you think you are doing?'

At first Hero didn't answer. His breaths were short and panicky. He looked down at the fabulous costume Jim had made him. He had known that sometime he was going to meet Pa or Ma or one of the others. And they would demand an explanation.

'I am a rat –' he said, haltingly – 'but I am different. I like humans.'

'You *what*?' Pa spluttered. He stood there, blinking. He could hardly believe his ears.

'I mean, some humans are nice to me. I like the

things that humans like.'

Pa looked as if he would explode. He seemed to puff his chest out and then deflate. This wasn't going too well.

'What *exactly* do you like?' Pa demanded.

'Sheets. Um. I like sheets. And soap. And fresh water. Being washed. And clothes.' They were the first things that came into Hero's mind.

'Sheets? Are you mad? Fresh water? Yuk! Eeeyuk – you're not a fish! And as for clothes. I mean, *clothes* are *unthinkable*! Don't you miss the lovely dirt? The dank, the rank, the fetid and the rancid? Eh? I like to sleep in a big pile of garbage – fleas jumping from stench to vaporous stench! That's the way to live. It's a rat thing. Is that not good enough for you? You like *clean* things? You like . . . *soap*?' He spat the word out in disgust. He was trembling. Worse, he was standing up on his hind legs with his paws on his hips, in a most un rat-like position. He quickly went flat. On all fours. Like a proper rat.

'Yes,' replied Hero defiantly. 'I do. Jim – the cabin boy – he saved me, Pa. And he looks after me, and talks and strokes me.'

'*Strokes* you?' repeated Pa. He was so horrified that he pulled a whisker out. 'OW! That is *disgusting*!

You have become his plaything. Have you no thought of us – your family? Have you no pride?' He waved his fine long whisker around.

Hero felt suddenly close to tears. He tried again to explain that he was different. 'I do think of you – but what you are . . . is different from me. I am experiencing life – like you said. I like dancing and sword-fighting and doing some human things! I'm learning from them. I'm even learning to under-stand their language. Maybe one day I could speak like them. That's what I want. That's life . . .'

'You are a RAT!' shouted Pa, losing his temper and flinging his whisker away. 'You're not a human. You're not a pet! You are a selfish rat! That's the only thing you share with humans! Selfishness! That's it, Hero – I'm finished with you. I disown you. I'm going back to my bilge water and my rotting veg-etables and one day we will find the sleepy lagoons of the Tropics – where the stink makes your whiskers curl – and we shall be *without you*!'

Pa turned and ran before Hero could say any-thing more. He was too upset to continue, and he could hear the boy returning. He had said what he wanted to say. Pa had seen what he had to see.

Hero felt a little tear welling up. He blinked it

away and took a deep breath of salty sea air. He couldn't help his feelings: if he liked being clean, and wearing clothes . . . well, why shouldn't he? The boy was his friend. The boy had saved him. He would be safer with the boy than stuck under the deck with all the others, in the darkness. There might be a price to pay, and maybe it would be bigger than he could bear – but he would do what he wanted to do. And he couldn't help thinking – secretly – (for he knew it was wrong and he tried not to think it) that he was better than the other rats.

Chapter Twenty-one
The Parents Suffer

Pa raged.

As he stalked away from Hero, his blood was boiling. Usually he would scurry furtively across the deck, keeping to the sides, taking care not to be seen – but now he marched boldly, openly across the deck, past the pig, Blossom, and down the hatch steps, his mind in turmoil.

He looked in at Spurdle, stirring a pot of broth, and considered attacking him. He could bite his ankle, at least? Sink his teeth into that bony leg. Spurdle was the cause of this. Spurdle and that cat.

But he decided against biting the cook – he would only get hurt – and marched down another

set of steps to the gun deck. He would like to train a cannon on to Spurdle and Jim and that cat and fire it. Booooom.

'Well?' asked Ma, when he reached the store-room.

Pa took a breath and steadied himself. He didn't want to cause any worry. 'He is a stubborn rat,' he declared, climbing on to one of the kegs. 'He is experimenting with life. Not very sensibly – but still – adventurously.'

'Oh? How adventurously?'

Pa groaned. 'He is dressed up like a peacock.'

Ma gave a little cry. 'Oh.'

The little rats sniggered.

'And he is dancing around with a sword.'

The little rats guffawed.

'It is not funny,' Pa told them gravely. 'He has gone utterly . . . mad. I think . . . he thinks he is a human.'

'A human?' shrieked Ma.

'Yes.'

'But he is . . . too hairy.'

'He has covered his hair up – with clothes.'

'Well. There are other things as well. He's too small, he's the wrong shape, he's got claws, different teeth, different brain, a tail, whiskers . . .'

Pa looked at her oddly. She didn't need to tell *him* that Hero was a rat. 'I know he is a rat. He's just . . . confused.'

'Oh dear,' Ma said, biting her lip. 'What are we to do?'

Pa scrambled up the little barrel to their nest, and burrowed in head first. He covered his head in straw and his anger subsided into misery. It would be nice to be swallowed up in sleep. To wake up to a fetid lagoon, with rotting vegetation bobbing around in it. He sighed, then summoned up his energy and called out to Ma, in a valiant attempt to be positive, 'Perhaps it is just a phase he is going through. A phase we have to endure. Hero has stopped experiencing life – now he is experimenting with it!'

Chapter Twenty-two
Touché

A week passed and Hero held the boy's finger with two paws and let himself be lifted up on to his hind legs. His feet were tired and aching. They were not made for standing upright. They weren't made for dancing or sword-fighting either. And the hat kept falling into his eyes.

He had spent most of the day in the boy's pocket. It was a dangerous place to be. Jim nearly sat on him twice. For safety, Hero curled himself up into a ball whenever Jim was moving around, because if Jim bumped into something, or someone bumped into Jim, he could be squashed.

He ate the raisins and biscuits that Jim dropped

into the pocket but it wasn't long before he felt terribly thirsty. The boy had forgotten that a rat needs water. Hero found the clothes hot. The jacket, trousers and hat were strange to him. Gorgeous, yes – but his fur was so much cooler. And when the clothes got wet, from the spray of a wave, the water soaked straight into them, making them damp and heavy. Water usually just ran off his fur, he thought wistfully.

Still, he did like the dancing and the swordplay. There was something elegant about it, and he flattered himself that he was good at it.

'Forward one-two. Back one-two,' urged Jim. Jim knew this rat was special. No one had ever seen a dancing rat before. Jim was excited and amazed. This was more than a pet – it was his chance to make his fortune. He began to guard Hero ever more closely.

Several times a day, Jim brought Hero below deck and set him on the top of a barrel and taught him to sword-fight and to dance. Shadows played across the wall as, late into the night, Hero held on to Jim's finger and waltzed back and forth, his paws gripping on to the finger and his snout in the air.

In the light of the lantern he jabbed and swirled

with his little sword, fighting the boy's finger. In addition to the silver jacket, Jim made him a red cape, cut from a flag, and it flew out behind Hero as he lunged and parried. Every few minutes Jim gave Hero a raisin.

Jim sewed buttons on to his pocket to protect Hero from falling out. It was hot and dark in there now. But the buttons also meant that even if he wanted to, Hero could not easily get out.

Days passed, and the training continued. Rocco the rat, as Jim called Hero, became better and stronger, until one evening, Jim called all the sailors together to tell them of his little pet.

'I have a special thing that I think you'll be liking to see,' he announced. He put his hand in his pocket and brought out Rocco the rat. He placed Hero on the barrel top.

The sailors laughed to see the little rodent dressed up in the clothes of a gentleman. Fifteen faces crowded around the barrel, chuckling and pointing.

'Watch!' Jim told them. In the hush, he held out his finger. 'En garde, Rocco.'

Hero stood up and held out the little sword. There were gasps of amazement. Jim came forward

with his finger, probing and prodding. Hero jabbed at the thick finger, swished this way and that and finally pricked it.

'Bravo!' the men shouted.

'Ouch!' Jim withdrew his finger. Hero settled back on all fours, panting. The sailors roared with laughter. They'd never seen anything like it. They craned their necks to get a better look. Hero felt the thrill of the crowd filling him up with excitement.

Now Jim produced a little sword of his own. And holding it between his thumb and forefinger, he advanced on the little rat, swirling and twirling the tiny sword. Hero fought the hand and the sword, beating it back, leading it on, jabbing again and again at the thick fingers. He liked the play–acting. He liked the amazed human faces peering down at him in admiration. This was splendid fun.

Beyond the pool of light, behind the sailors, no one saw six little rats running up a mast and sitting on a wooden spar above the action. From their vantage point, Ma and Pa looked on in dismay.

'Look – oh my, oh my.' Pa closed his eyes and shook his head.

'He's not in danger, is he?' asked Ma, thinking

perhaps it was a funny sort of dance.

'No,' said Chewy, grinning at the spectacle.

'Stab him!' cried Happy.

'Jab him!' cried Solo.

'He is in danger,' Pa lamented. 'He has become their toy. They can do what they want with him.'

'But they don't want to kill him, do they?' Ma asked.

'Maybe not. But look at him: he has crossed over to their side. He really thinks he is more human than rat. He'll be drinking rum and eating with a knife and fork soon. He has betrayed us. He has betrayed his species!'

'Oh, but he doesn't mean to,' said Ma. She couldn't help indulging him – she was his mother after all.

'Look what I got!' a voice snarled on the deck below them. The sailors turned. It was Spurdle. He was holding Menace the cat, high up in the air. 'Menace will give your filthy little rat a run for his money!' He pushed through the crowd of sailors and held the cat over the barrel. Her green eyes glinted in the lamplight. When she saw the little rat, she stiffened and craned her head forward to get at it.

Jim snatched Hero up and held him safe.

The sailors were divided. Half of them wanted the little rat to fight the cat – the other half thought it was unfair.

'It's no contest. That cat will rip the little fella to pieces,' said one.

'It will be a good fight,' laughed another.

'A little sword is no match for a cat's claws,' cried Jim.

'Darling!' shrieked Ma, seeing Spurdle thrust the cat close to Hero and laugh horribly as he did it. Ma tried to leap from the spar.

Pa grasped Ma's tail to hold her back. The cat hissed at Hero, stretching her claws and baring her teeth, and pushing forward eagerly. Hero shrank back.

'I'll fight that cat!' shouted Ma.

'Shhhh,' Pa told her.

'Get away!' Jim turned from the cook and shielded Hero in his shirt. He wasn't going to let the cat near his prized possession.

'We'll have it out later, lad.' Spurdle narrowed his eyes at the boy. He turned and walked away, suddenly tossing the cat on to the deck as if she were a rubber ball. In the air Menace twisted round and landed neatly on all fours. She ran back to the barrel, to see if there was still a rat to catch.

'What are we going to do?' Ma turned to her mate.

Pa's nose twitched. 'Nothing,' he said. 'Hero has made his choice: to be all human and dressed up like that. He has to live with it.'

Ma's lip curled. Her whiskers bristled. 'I'm going to talk with him,' she said.

Chapter Twenty-three
Humans v. Animals

Hero lay in Jim's hammock, resting in the sheets. He felt strange. *Is this loneliness?* he wondered. After the triumph of his appearance before the sailors, he felt somehow let down, empty. Yet how enjoyable it had been to be surrounded by happy, cheering human faces.

But he was bothered by something. He couldn't get the image of Menace out of his mind. Those sharp teeth. Those huge, green eyes. Menace's eyes were sly, but they were desperate to fight. Greedy to kill him.

What have I ever done to that cat? Hero wondered, swaying gently in the stuffy sleeping quarters. *Can't*

she see that I am wearing clothes? I'm practically a human. Hero felt mildly insulted that Menace still wanted to attack him.

'Pssssst!'

He looked up. 'Ma!' he cried, seeing his mother's face at the hole above the hammock.

'Hello, darling.' Ma sniffed the air and then dropped deftly on to the canvas hammock. She looked at Hero and shook her head. He was lounging on a little cushion still dressed in his ridiculous finery.

'You silly boy,' Ma began, coming immediately to the point. 'I don't know what you think you're doing, dancing up there for all those humans. It is the strangest thing I've ever seen a rat do. It's unnatural. It's extraordinary.'

Hero studied his cuffs. He didn't want to hear this. Why couldn't he do what he wanted to do? Why couldn't they leave him to make his own mistakes? These cuffs were very pretty, even though they got in the way of his claws.

'Pa says you like human things. I can't think why.' Ma blinked at him.

Hero felt uncomfortable. He tried to explain. 'I suppose because they're better than us. They have ships and tools and clothes and clever language. I can learn from them.'

Ma felt confused. What a fiercely independent rat this was. It was difficult having such a bright and thoughtful and yet wayward child.

'But their things are for them – not us,' she ventured.

'But if an animal came to the humans that was better than the humans, wouldn't the humans learn from that animal?'

Ma wondered. She twirled her tail and she waggled her whiskers. 'It's a big thought,' she said, feeling defeated.

'I like big thoughts,' said Hero rather grandly.

'It's not nice to be a pet,' Ma told him.

'Why not? I get fed, and clothed. I have a place to live. Like Blossom the pig, I am, and though you may find it hard to believe, I am actually loved.'

'But I love you too! And you are not loved – you are *owned*.' Ma had never been a great one for arguments but these suddenly seemed so right. She felt inspired. 'You don't belong to yourself. You belong to your owner. Hero, you're not *free*.'

'What is so great about being free?' asked Hero.

Ma blinked. She didn't know how to explain it.

'You . . . you make your own decisions. You do what you want. You are responsible for yourself. That's good.'

Hero curled his lip. 'I can leave anytime I like,' he said.

Ma opened her mouth to say more, but they heard a sudden commotion up above.

'I must go,' she said quickly. 'Take care, my Hero.' She deftly took a leap up to the hole above the hammock, managed to grip her claw on the edge, and hauled herself up. From the safety of the hole in the ceiling, she looked down, a fondness in her eyes.

'Bye,' she said simply.

Chapter Twenty-four
Pig for the Pot

Hero lay and thought about what Ma had said. He missed her — but then he told himself that he was growing up and he had to become independent. He had to grow up and grow away from her and the family, didn't he?

On deck he heard more commotion: raised voices and squealing. He jumped up and went to investigate. As he hurried through the rat runs, still dressed in his finery, he heard Oleg Olegovitch up above, protesting.

Arriving on the scene Hero was astonished. Oleg had his arms around Blossom's middle and Spurdle was above them holding a knife.

'Kill me first!' bellowed Oleg. 'Blossom is mine. Never will I have her killed. She is my beloved pig!'

'I has orders,' Spurdle told him. 'The pig is for the pot. She is smelling out the captain, and the paying passengers. The ladies don't like pigsty smell. More than that – she is good fresh food and we all need fresh food!'

'Aye!' cried the sailors.

'But I have nothing in the world,' wailed Oleg. 'My ship is lost. I am rescued by your good selves – but all my fortune is gone under the waves. You are putting me in the next port – so kind – but that is New Orleans! America! How am I to get back to Murmansk!'

Hero could not follow the argument. But he could see the knife held aloft in Spurdle's hand. He could read the evil intent. He felt for Blossom. He felt for Oleg. He admired Oleg for protecting Blossom. How noble it was!

'Sire,' said a soft Scottish voice.

Everyone on deck turned. Though the voice was soft, it had a commanding authority. Captain McNeeps stepped forth from the shadows and addressed Oleg. McNeeps stood tall, his red beard gently ruffled by the wind, the buttons on his smart coat shining.

'Captain Olegovitch, you must be reasonable. And in return I shall be reasonable. The pig, sire, is a burden to this vessel. She eats too much, she smells too much, she grunts too much. Of course – she is a pig, so I do not hold it against her. But I have seen the hungry looks in my sailors' eyes. That pig is fresh meat. She is roast pork. She is ham. She is bacon.'

'She is my pig!' wailed Oleg.

'Indeed. But I ask you: have you paid your passage? Have you paid for the passage of the pig?'

Oleg was silent.

'No. And you have nothing to pay with. Listen: I shall pay you for this pig. Money. Enough for you to get back to Murmansk if you work part of your passage.'

Hero stared at the scene. He could sense a shift in the argument. He could see the glint in Spurdle's eye.

Oleg stared at the captain. It was a good offer. It was money. Money to take him home. And home was where he wanted to be. He began to nod his head slowly.

'Sorry, Bloss.' He stood up and hung his head.

'The pig – for money – you may have her.' Oleg spoke quietly and he stepped away without a backward glance.

So quickly! The human abandoned the thing he loved! Hero watched as Blossom was hauled away, squealing. The sailors cheered – but Hero felt a desperate gloom pressing down upon him.

He slunk back to the hammock and curled up in the sheets. He didn't understand what had happened, but he knew that he didn't like it. If only he could understand more of their language, it might make more sense. Why had Oleg walked away and stopped protecting Blossom? Hadn't he said he loved the pig?

Chapter Twenty-five
Trapped

Later that night, as the smells of roast pork wafted through the ship, Jim came into the sleeping quarters carrying something behind his back. He placed it on the floor under the hammock. Hero lay resting in his sheets. Jim found Hero and picked him up, gently but firmly.

'Hello, Rocco, me old mate,' he said. Hero looked into Jim's eyes. They were glinting darkly.

Jim took down the lantern that was swinging above them on a beam. He bent back down to the floor again.

Now Jim held Hero in front of the object he had brought in. It was covered with a black cloth. All of a sudden, Hero didn't trust Jim. Blossom shouldn't have trusted Oleg, and he shouldn't trust Jim. Humans had other ideas. Ideas he couldn't understand. He struggled, but Jim kept a firm hold of him.

'It is all right, Rocco,' he said softly. 'I have this from the captain. Look. It's a present.' With a flourish, Jim pulled off the cover to reveal . . . a cage.

Hero looked at the cage. He wanted to cry out in anguish. It was made of wire and it had a little swing like a trapeze swaying in the middle. The bottom was lined with straw. There was something sinister about it. He saw that it was designed to take away his freedom in a moment.

Struggling with his feelings, Hero tried to communicate in the way the humans did. 'Why?' he asked. It came out as a squeak.

Jim grinned. 'Oh, Rocco! Are you talking to me?' he asked. 'This is for the best, I promise.'

'I don't want to live in here!' Hero squeaked again – but he realised that he made no sense to Jim. He couldn't speak Jim's language, would never speak Jim's language, because he couldn't make a human sound. There really were limits.

Jim lifted Hero through the little door, into the

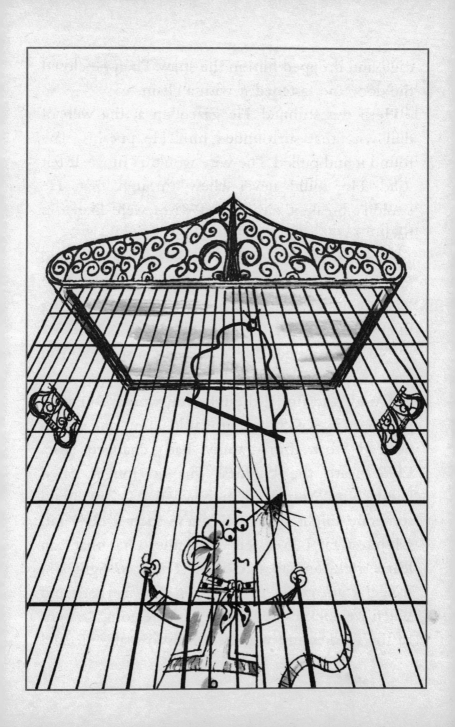

cage, and dropped him in the straw. Then he closed the door and fastened it with a chain.

Hero was stunned. He gazed up at the web of dull wire that surrounded him. He put his claw round it and pulled. The wire wouldn't move. It felt solid. He could never chew through that. He couldn't break it either. The wires were like iron bars.

He ran around the cage. Two steps one way and four steps the other.

'Do you like your new home?' asked Jim, peering in at him.

'No,' Hero cried. But it was only a squeak. 'You can't put me in here. I hate it!'

'Good,' said Jim. 'I thought you would. You are a precious rat, y'know,' Jim told him and Hero noticed that Jim's tone had changed too. Underneath the kindness Jim no longer cared about him. 'You're so precious that I am afraid someone might steal you. You're such a *clever* rat. Cleverest rat I ever seen. Imagine: a rat that can learn tricks and wear clothes! That can fight and dance! I am going to keep you safe in there and when we dock at New Orleans, we're going straight to the market and you are going to make money!

So much money – you wouldn't believe! You're going to make me rich.' Jim's eyes were wide with greed. 'I shall make you dance and fight and people will pay and pay again to see you – and then I will sell you to the highest bidder!'

Hero looked up at Jim. He didn't understand everything that the boy had said, but he understood enough. The boy didn't love him. The boy didn't want to be friends. The boy owned him and was going to sell him. The boy's eyes were greedy, and Hero recoiled from them.

Jim hung the cage from a nail in the ceiling. When he climbed into his hammock, the cage swung level with his face. Jim smiled in at the little rat.

'You're safe,' he said. 'The cat will never get you in there.' He pushed a raisin through the bars and whispered, 'Goodnight.'

Hero ate the raisin slowly. He was growing tired of raisins. He hoped Ma and Pa weren't watching. He lay in the straw and covered his face. It was hot and sticky, and smelled of bird. This wasn't a rat's cage – if such a thing existed – it was a cage for a songbird.

What a fool – to have trusted the boy! To have

believed that all the dancing and sword-fighting were fun. What a fool he was to have pretended to be a human! He took off his hat and his cape and he flung them down in the straw. All his proud words to Ma sounded empty now.

He moved over to the cage door and tried it again. It was tight shut with the twisted wire. He managed to find the ends of the wire, but his little paws were not strong enough to untwist it. After a minute of so of trying, he gave up.

He was a rat, he told himself. He was not a human. He was a rat. Pa was right – he had become a toy to please the humans. He lay down and closed his eyes and tried to think of sweeter times.

Chapter Twenty-six
Cat Fight

In the middle of the night, Hero's cage was quietly lifted off the hook and Hero woke up, feeling the swinging movement of the cage. He glimpsed the sleeping form of Jim as the cage swung down, and then he saw light from a lantern shining into his cage. For a moment he thought someone had come to rescue him – then, peeping through the straw, to his surprise, Hero saw the grey, unshaven face of the cook, Spurdle.

'Now we shall have us some sport,' Spurdle hissed. His eyes flashed in the lamplight and his yellow teeth were bared at the little rat. Hero trembled.

With the lantern in one hand and the cage in the other, Spurdle nimbly weaved past the hammocks and the snoring sailors. At the door, he stepped over the threshold and then scuttled through the dark ship, down a flight of steps to the galley.

Menace was curled up asleep on a cushion, but Spurdle nudged her with his foot and she woke up instantly. He bent down and showed her the cage.

'Look, my lovely: the fighting rat! There he is looking so pleased with himself. He needs a lesson taught to him, eh? Do you agree?'

The cat purred so loudly that the cage vibrated. Strings of saliva dripped from Menace's mouth. She wrapped her tail round Spurdle's legs and weaved in and out in a slinky embrace. She would fight this rat; she would take it slowly, toy with it, tease it, enjoy it. Hero felt a cold sweat breaking out over his body but also a strength, because he knew that he was going to fight and maybe that meant there was a chance.

Snatching up the cage, Spurdle turned and left the galley, confident that the cat would follow. He scuttled through the darkness, deeper into the ship – down to the gun deck – he wanted to be in a secret place, away from the prying eyes of shipmates who might not like what he was doing.

Menace followed close on his heels. Spurdle took a key from his pocket and opened a door. The room was marked 'Danger'.

Inside lay kegs of gunpowder stacked up one on the other. As they entered, there was a scratching and a scurrying, and Menace suddenly shot forward trying to catch a thin tail that disappeared round the back of one of the kegs.

'Hah – the vermin are here, eh?' Spurdle muttered. 'Crafty beasts.'

Hero suddenly recognised the smell and the noises. He heard a familiar mewling. Was this . . . Was this where the family had built a nest, he wondered. His hopes rose – surely his family would help him. If they all attacked together . . .

Spurdle placed the cage on top of a crate. Menace sprang up beside it and prowled around the cage, her purring bursting with eagerness. Hero crouched in the straw, thoughts rushing through his head. *What did Jim say? I'll look after you. What did Pa say? Be a rat. Be crafty. Seize life.*

Hero picked up the sword. If Spurdle put the cat in the cage, Hero would have to be quick. He would have to fight. Surprise would be good. He must surprise the cat. If Spurdle took him out of the cage, then he would have to run, run for his life.

He waited. The cook undid the cage door. Hero held the sword in his quivering paw. The cook began to reach in, and Hero gripped the sword tightly, ready to pounce, to bite, to run . . .

But the cook had second thoughts. He didn't want his hand bitten by the filthy rat. Menace tried to push her head through the cage door − but Spurdle stopped her.

'Wait,' he growled.

Now Spurdle grasped the doorway to the cage in one hand and with a powerful wrench peeled back one entire side of the cage. The wire joints snapped and pinged as he pulled it apart. Hero was horrified: he was now completely exposed.

Spurdle held the cat, gripping the soft skin behind her neck. Hero was trembling from head to tail. He beheld Menace, a hissing, snarling ball of fur and claws . . . and then he saw Spurdle let her go.

In moments of great stress and great danger, time is said to slow down. So it did now for Hero. What took a matter of seconds felt like a lifetime. As the cat came forward, Hero held out the sword. It struck Menace's jaw and broke uselessly.

The cat snarled in pain and, at the same moment,

Hero ran up the side of the cage to the top. As he twisted round, Menace lashed out with her claw, her lethal talons splayed like curved surgeon's needles on the end of her paw. She caught Hero's jacket – the jacket Jim had given him – and flung him to the ground. For a moment Menace held him there. Pinned. Seconds from death.

Hero struggled and wriggled.

'Bite his head off, Menace,' Spurdle urged the grinning cook.

Hero swivelled and shrank from the huge cat looming over him and suddenly tore free of the jacket, squeezing out of it, leaving Menace with the silvery material stuck to her claw. *You can wriggle out of clothes – but not out of your fur*, Hero thought. It gave him a vital second. He turned – and glimpsed faces in the shadows.

It was his family! Pa and Ma and Chewy and Solo and Happy and Morgan. They seemed to be poised, ready to pounce! Hero saw immediately that he must lead the cat towards them.

He scrambled off the keg, almost smashed into Spurdle's lantern on the floor, and sprinted their way.

A moment later Menace sprang. She smashed into the lantern, yowling, and Spurdle cried out in alarm. There was a flash of light as Hero squeezed to safety between two barrels, and shrank into the darkness, shaking.

Only it wasn't darkness. All around him there was light. Spurdle was cursing — hopping up and down and beating the flames. The lantern had spilled its oil and was burning out across the floor.

'GET OUT!' shouted Pa, rushing past Hero. 'Quick, follow me! Get out, get out. Fire fire!'

'Oh, my darling, you were wonderful!' cried Ma and fell upon Hero and hugged him.

'Come ON!' Pa urged desperately.

The rats rushed past, grabbing Hero as they went and pulling him along. They squeezed through a hole in the floor and then quickly down, down and away.

They fled along a rat run to the front of the ship.

'The place is full of powder,' cried Pa, as they ran along. 'Fire on a wooden ship. Fire in the powder room! Oh! Fire is dangerous. Quickly! Come on!' he urged. Other rats were now joining them, appearing out of the darkness and rushing to the bows.

And Pa thought again of puddings. Stewed plums and custard, apple pie and cream.

'What is the powder?' asked Morgan, mystified.

'Gunpowder,' said Pa.

Chapter Twenty-seven
Then . . .

K ABBBBBOOOOOOMMMMM!

The ship blew up.

Chapter Twenty-eight
Survivors

In one ten-thousandth of a second, the stern of the ship splintered into two million pieces. The mast came down with a crash on deck. The rudder hung loosely in the water. The sea poured in. Black smoke mushroomed up over the sea.

All across the ship, voices cried out in panic. A fire in the powder room was a disaster, a calamity. Captain McNeeps was still wearing his pyjamas. He wasted no time.

'Passengers to the lifeboats! All hands to the fire! You — fetch sand buckets! You — bail water! You — launch the boats!'

Ma and Pa and the little rats ran to the bows of the ship. They had to run uphill because the bows were rising as the stern was sinking. They didn't want to be caught in the hold as the ship went down, so Pa led them up to the deck.

'The lifeboats! We have to get to the lifeboats!' Ma was hopping up and down desperately. They looked back down the sloping deck. Half of the ship had been destroyed. The sailors and passengers were struggling to climb into the lifeboats. All around them rats were emerging from inside the ship. They knew instinctively that the ship was sinking.

'Look at all our relatives!' squeaked Chewy.

'Where have they been?' asked Morgan. 'I never knew there were so many!'

'Is that Marion?' said Pa, squinting towards the lifeboat.

'It is. She's waving!' said Ma.

Bold as brass Marion was hanging from the pocket of the fur coat Oleg Olegovitch was carrying. She waved.

'Come on,' cried Chewy. 'Let's join her.'

'No,' Pa held him back. 'It's too far away. We must find something else.'

'Pa.' Solo's voice was flat and she was staring straight ahead. 'Pa!' she said again.

The rats followed her gaze.

Coming out of the hatch was a black furry animal. Menace. She had survived the blast. Her fur was singed, her eyes were bloodshot and blazing.

'Oh my dear!' cried Ma, clinging to Pa.

Pa backed away. He stood between the cat and his family. The rats shrank back as one body. But Menace had seen them and was slowly advancing. She moved with a limp.

'I thought she would be dead,' said Ma, trembling.

'Just one of her nine lives.' Pa gulped. He thought of puddings again. The end was near. This black beast was a killer. She would do for them – or the sinking ship would. What a place to build a nest – behind a keg of gunpowder! His stupidity was quite unbelievable.

The rats edged backwards. They stepped on each other's tails. It was awkward going backwards, but they had to watch the cat. The cat stalked them, slowly, menacingly. She prowled towards them, crouching low. Her prey was trapped. She was going to make them suffer slowly.

'Where's Hero?' asked Ma, counting her little ones.

Pa kept his eyes locked to the green eyes of Menace. He noticed that she had lost her whiskers – perhaps burned by the fire. 'What do you mean?' he whispered. 'He was with us, wasn't he?'

'He's not with us now,' said Happy.

'Typical,' Chewy huffed.

The rats retreated further and further until they reached the very front of the ship. They had no choice. Menace was cornering them, enjoying this slow capture, wondering which to pick off first. She didn't want a single one of these vermin to escape.

At the very front of the ship lay the bowsprit. It was a long wooden pole and stretched out over the figurehead of the lion with the fish in its mouth. The lion was a grim inspiration to Menace – the lion was the golden king of the cats. Menace was his deadly shadow.

There was nowhere else to go. As the sun blinked over the horizon, the rats edged along the narrow bowsprit. Around them the smoke from the ship turned orange in the dawn.

At the end of the bowsprit there was only air and a drop to the deep sea. All together the rats retreated along the bowsprit, glancing down at the ocean swell.

'What's that?' asked Solo, squinting out across the water.

There was a dark line that seemed to stretch into the sky.

Pa peered across the sea and almost lost his footing. 'Whoa! It's a ship!' he exclaimed.

'No, it's not – it's too big,' said Ma.

Pa squinted again. 'It's a great big fish – no – a whale – NO . . . it's a mountain! It's a mountain! It's LAND!'

'We've arrived!' squealed Happy and did a daring little jump.

'Just one little problem,' said Solo. She looked at Menace. Everyone fell silent. It was a big problem.

'The horrid beast is smiling.' Ma shuddered as Menace took a step on to the bowsprit. Her purring was like a roll of drums heralding a public event.

'Let's rush her!' suggested Chewy. 'She may get some of us, but others might make it.'

'Or we could push her off,' said Happy. 'Look at her limp.'

'Or fall ourselves,' Morgan whined.

Back they went, away from the cat, until they reached the very end of the bowsprit. There was no further to go. They clung to the narrow wooden spar as the cat licked her lips and prepared to pounce.

'What would you say was the very best pudding of all?' asked Pa, out of the blue. He knew now this really was the end.

'Treacle pudding,' everyone replied.

Pa had to agree.

'Summer pudding!' shouted a little voice below them.

Ma and Pa and the little rats looked down into the blue ocean. A plank of wood was bobbing towards them and on the plank a wet and pathetic little figure. It was Hero.

'Come on!' he shouted. 'Jump!'

'Hero!' shouted his little brothers and sisters. They needed no more encouragement − indeed there was nowhere else to go. 'Weeeeee' they all cried and together they leaped into the sea.

Plop-plop-plop-plop.

'Come back,' shouted Ma, and threw herself after them.

'Eh?' It was too fast for Pa. He was on his own

now. Face to face with Menace.

Menace opened her mouth. Pa gazed into the red cavern beyond the sharp white teeth.

'Come on, Pa!' cried the little ones from below.

With a whoop of triumph, Pa launched himself into the void.

'Sticky toffee pudding!' he sang, as he sailed through the air.

Chapter Twenty-nine
Surf Rats

Coughing and spluttering, the rats scrambled on board the plank and mobbed Hero, smothering him with kisses and shaking the water off their coats. They were so excited that they pushed him off and they all tumbled into the water again, laughing with relief. Pa was the last to get on.

'Move over,' he spluttered, having swallowed half a tot of sea-water. He belched. 'What an idea! What a perfect idea! I'd have thought of it myself, only . . .'

'My Hero,' said Ma.

The plank of wood began to drift away from the ship. Above them Menace crouched on the bowsprit. She could see the rats on the plank . . . but she was frightened of water. She couldn't swim. It was certain death. The hateful, rotten low-down dirty rats could swim! It was not right.

Now Menace had to find a way out. The bowsprit was pointing higher into the sky as the stern of the ship sank lower and lower in the sea. Menace backed off the bowsprit. Beaten.

Behind them, the rats heard humans shouting. The sailors and passengers were crowding into the lifeboats.

'Paddle the plank. Paddle the plank. Paddle the plank,' the rats cried.

The rats took it in turns to paddle the plank. The sun was warm now and the dark waters turned a beautiful turquoise blue.

'It never occurred to me that a plank of wood would make such a good craft,' considered Pa.

Hero smiled. 'It's a tool,' he said quietly.

Pa blinked in the bright sunlight, and licked his salty lips. Humans used tools, not rats. Hero was right. Hero had learned from the humans. He had to admit . . . that was crafty.

'You are a crafty old rat,' he said affectionately.

Hero couldn't help smiling. He was back in the family fold, where he belonged. He knew he wasn't a human. And he knew he never wanted to be a human's pet (though he would argue, there were *some* good things about being a pet). Nevertheless he had proved that they could learn from humans, there was no doubt about it.

'No experiences are wasted, when you live life to the full,' he told his father.

Pa nodded. He could have said that himself!

'Are there sharks in these waters?' asked Ma presently.

'Probably,' Pa said. It made him dizzy to look down.

'What's a shark?' asked Morgan.

'It's a fish,' Pa told him.

'Sharks like to eat humans not rats, Morgan,' Ma told him.

Behind them, a slow creaking noise reached them and the ship – quite far away now – keeled over and slipped under the surface of the sea. It was gone. Away off to their left, lifeboats carried the humans – and some crafty rats – to the shore.

'Where are we?' asked Chewy.

Pa sniffed the air. There was a sweetness, a fragrant rotting of vegetation; a delicious warmth that thrilled his sensitive nose. In the distance he could just make out a long stretch of sandy beach where palm trees crowded down to the water's edge.

He felt a huge feeling of satisfaction filling him up. It was the pleasure of achievement, of dangers overcome, of journeys finishing, of things learned and life lived, of children growing up, a feeling expanding inside him and filling him up with happiness. This was a moment to savour; even the elements conspired to make him happy: the swell lifted the plank up, to give them a better view of the bay.

'I do believe,' he announced, savouring every second of the moment of the announcement, 'that –'

No one was paying him any attention. They were looking past him. Open-mouthed. Pa turned to follow their gaze and saw the most enormous wave, a cliff of water, as big as a terrace of houses, rearing up above them, its dripping mouth about to swallow them whole . . .

'Oh, my crafty cousins . . .'

From that moment on the Morgan Street Rats surely thought of themselves as the *luckiest* rats in the world. As the wave rose, it did not suck them under into its deadly turbulence, but instead it

swept them up on to its crest and they rode the surf, standing up, at terrific, astonishing speed, through a cascading tunnel of water, past the roiling foam of the surf, smoothly on to the beach.

It was a miracle.

'As I was saying,' said Pa, stepping on to the white sand of the beach, his voice smaller and humbler than a moment before, 'this is the Tropics.'

The rats flopped on to the sand.

'I never want to board another ship, as long as I live,' said Ma.

Pa put his snout in the air.

'I smell rubbish,' he said, grinning.